Kill Me Why?

RITU SETHI

Kill Me Why?

Chief Inspector Gray James Detective
Mystery Series Book 2

GRAY JAMES BOOK 3: COMING SOON

FOR EXCLUSIVE CONTENT~SUBSCRIBE AT

www.rituwrites.com

CONTENTS

GET NOTIFIED WHEN BOOK 3 IS RELEASED
ON PROMOTIONAL PRICE:

SUBSCRIBE

www.rituwrites.com

For Jacob

CHAPTER ONE

ON SATURDAY, December 23, Chief Inspector Gray James unknowingly drove towards the Stitcher's third crime scene.

"Tell me where we're going," he said to his passenger.

"No, not yet."

"Why?"

"I'm afraid you might say no. And you're needed on this case."

"Then I may as well turn this car around now."

"No, you won't. Your curiosity would take you off the edge of a cliff. Don't worry. That won't happen today."

Driving across dark mountainous roads, jostling headlights flashing upon moss-covered boulders, towering pines, and occasional startled feral eyes in the bushes, Gray kept his meditative calm, held at bay the gloom which occasionally threatened to consume him.

Ordinarily, his passenger, forensic pathologist John Seymour, was a proverbial fountain of bubbling information. He liked nothing better than stepping past the confines of his job and accompanying Gray on cases – and yet now he sat stolidly in the passenger seat of the Lotus Exige, his round silver-rimmed glasses sitting below thick blond brows resembling caterpillars trying to jump off his face.

The thrashing Pacific and the town of Halfmoon Bay lay miles below, as did Gray's family seaside cabin, just a few hours from Vancouver along British Columbia's ironically named Sunshine Coast.

Christmas in coastal Halfmoon epitomized charm. The streets were decked with illuminated sleighs, decorated trees, and lights adorning quaint shops: the local butcher, the elegant bistro-café, Rusty's pie and home decorations, and Stone Art Gallery, frequented by tourists and featuring local and national sculptors and painters.

With every passing kilometer, Gray travelled further from that charm and up into the wild BC Mountains he adored. Wafts of birch and pine brought back visceral teenage memories – of hiking these trails with Dad, making coffee on the camping stove, hungrily ripping home-dried beef jerky with his teeth. Yet he knew that something sinister and unnatural awaited – as it always did with his job.

"It's not my jurisdiction," Gray said, swerving on a hairpin turn. The cliff's edge was only a meter to the right.

"Won't matter, James." The doctor always called him by his last name, a habit from years of working together on the force. "Just wait and see."

"Remind me never to invite you over for the holidays again. Why are you grinning?"

"I've just never seen you without your thousand dollar suit. You seem almost human."

A few tricky turns, directed at the last minute by Seymour, brought them to their mystery destination.

No sign adorned the iron gate which autonomously opened and shut behind them. No intercom voice greeted their arrival.

The Lotus's wheels rolled over grass and spat mud while edging along a claustrophobic, winding trail barely wide enough for the car. Branches scratched against the custom teal finish, grinding at Gray's insides.

He gave Seymour a dark sideways glance – to which the doctor merely shrugged.

Finally, the trail ended, and they reached a dimly lit patch of ground, flanked by a border of trees to the left, and low-lying mist to the right. Only a single, beat-up pickup rested in this makeshift car park. Gray pulled up beside it.

The drenched ground squished and slid under his feet as though it were alive.

He pulled together the collar of his black leather jacket against the wind and inhaled the cold, wet air – tinged with the smell of something else... something very wrong.

Seymour stepped out of the car. He was tall but not as tall as Gray. "What do you think?"

"I think my loafers will never be the same."

The doctor pointed towards the right, where, within a clearing patch of mist, an amorphous form was taking the shape of a rustic cabin. Smoke spiraled upward through the crumbling brick chimney, and a back-lit silhouette paced at the paned window.

"Alright," Gray said. "If this is the crime scene, where are the Scene of Crime Officers? I need more information before we proceed."

"I'd rather the lady inside tell you."

"Why the secrecy?"

"I'm not quite sure how you'll react to the details."

The doctor moved forward alongside Gray, their familiarity a balm against the storm. Although Gray mainly lived in the eye of that storm – calm, at peace – and watching the cyclone all around him with detached interest. It was a tough thing to admit to people who judged – who didn't know firsthand what he'd been through – but he was blissfully happy in Montreal before his wife's return. He suspected happier than he had a right to be given his son's death. He'd moved past loss to that sweet place where nothing that happened mattered because he had nothing left to lose.

Until recently. But he was determined to get there again. By the end of this vacation.

"You can't solve your problems in an instant," Seymour said, in his usual ironic tone.

"Three years isn't an instant."

"But you've just returned home to this –" he gestured with long, tapered fingers, "wilderness of yours. Although I can't imagine why."

"I hid these last three years in Montreal. I didn't know I had a –"

"Daughter?" Seymour completed. "Must have been a shock."

But this wasn't the time or place for this conversation. What the hell was this place?

"Did you see the tracks going up the mountain?" Gray said. "Before we turned into the gate?"

"What? No, I didn't see anything."

"Someone must have come out this way after this morning's rain."

The slamming of Seymour's car door must have announced their arrival because a tall young woman with streaming, almost witch-like, hair ran out the front door, then paused to take them both in before motioning them to follow her towards a darkened path to the right.

Seymour acknowledged her with a wave.

She'd moved so fast that Gray, who had, since childhood, categorized impressions into flavors, had only a fleeting impression of licorice (her hair), strawberries (the red lipstick on full lips), and vanilla (from her impossibly pale skin).

The woman evaporated into the murky blackness.

No introductions; no preliminaries. Only getting down to business, which suited Gray fine, since all he wanted was to get back to his Dad's cabin, put up his feet by the hearth, and have a drink – a single malt scotch to warm his chilled bones.

He scanned his smartwatch: it was just past ten.

Mud gripped his heels with each step. After about fifty feet, his nostrils screamed.

"That smell –"

"Try and ignore it," Seymour said, walking alongside him.

Now well past the cabin, Gray hesitated before entering the pitch dark – afraid of meeting that void within himself which made it hard to move from one moment to the next, from one breath to the next. Especially this last week of being back in his hometown – where the greatest tragedy of his life had happened. What if he stepped into that darkness and never came out? His heart slammed his ribs; breathing became a struggle. A panic he'd never known before threatened to consume him.

Gray shoved past it, arms outstretched, feet crunching over uneven ground, not knowing what lay before him, with only Seymour's raspy breathing by his side.

"Doctor –"

"Just a little further."

A click preceded a series of lights turning on, suddenly blinding, revealing a large rectangular patch illuminated by three oblong beams.

The woman had reached a spot adjacent to a wired fence on the far right, where a blue tarp covered the ground. It looked flat, as though covering nothing but dirt. Certainly no dead body lay under it.

She stood against the wind, the silk hair jetting behind her. Now Gray noticed that she appeared to be of mixed heritage: part South-Asian, part Caucasian? She was also gorgeous.

"I found it here," she.

Thick, cold droplets touched his cheeks. The full sky was giving way, having concealed the last of the overhead stars with low-lying clouds.

Seymour introduced the woman as Dr. Emerald Kaur, who responded with a firm handshake and eyes which couldn't quite meet Gray's.

Accustomed to a certain response from women, Gray noticed the unshielded resentment in her eyes with interest. He didn't mind; perhaps she distrusted all policemen.

"Sergeant Slope didn't believe me," she said.

"Slope's been here?"

"Yes. Earlier today."

Seymour had mentioned the word 'murder' to get Gray to come with him, but little else.

No signs identified the site, save brown, individually numbered markers placed close to the ground. He opened his mouth to ask, when Seymour said:

"Tell him about the corpse, Emmy."

Emmy?

"It's gone," she said.

Gray had already pieced that together by SOCO's absence. No Scene of Crime Officers likely meant the lack of a corpse. And with the local sergeant not believing "Emmy," that implied she'd seen something no one else had.

"Am I correct in assuming that the body disappeared when you went to go for help?" Gray said.

"Of course." She turned to Seymour. "Haven't you told him anything?"

"I thought this would be more fun."

Emmy sighed and began a robotic recital: "Every day at 3 pm, each body gets assessed by one of my student staff, or me. Today, I noticed a change at site 144 right away – a change in color."

"Color? I'm having difficulty following you." This place...this peculiar place – at once familiar yet foreign, with that awful smell –

She pinned him with a stare a professor might reserve for a not very promising student.

"Do you live or work here?" Gray asked. "You mentioned students and a site –"

He took in the scent, the seemingly scattered debris and site markings. And suddenly, without having ever visited one before, he'd knew where he was.

"Is this a body farm?"

"We don't call it that," Emmy snapped.

Seymour jumped in. "She's right; that's an ignorant layman's term."

"I'm only an ignorant policeman." Gray faced Seymour. "Why didn't you tell me this was a forensic research facility?"

"I'm a forensic pathologist. You could have worked it out yourself. Besides, curiosity got you off that chair by the fire and out here on a cold night, didn't it?" The doctor ran a thick-knuckled hand through his thinning hair. The caterpillar eyebrows rose a fraction and fell in conciliatory appeal. "A lot rides on you taking the case, unofficially."

Emmy unceremoniously pushed Seymour out of the way. "If I can continue?"

"Go right ahead."

"I found a specimen lying spread-eagled, long blond hair sprawled out in a fan, the neck bent at a peculiar angle. The

7

bright pink underwear initially caught my attention from afar, and, of course, I didn't reposition the corpse. I know better than to interfere with evidence."

She painted quite a picture. Gray took in his surroundings: the rusting dilapidated car with the closed trunk; the recycling bin resting against a towering maple with branches arching on either side as though anxiously guarding the contents; the irregularly lumpy garbage bag casually tossed by the nearby fence.

Each section of this so-called body farm possessed a sequential number.

He approached site 144 with a quickened pulse and a healthy amount of dread, his new shoes squishing in the soaked, rotting earth. Wetness seeped into the stitched seams and drenched his socks.

Emmy began a recital. "We observe and record the decomposition process in various circumstances. We study and form an understanding of the decompositional changes that occur in the human body and use that research for medical, legal, and educational purposes."

"And this," he pointed to a mannequin-like leg sticking up from the ground at site 144, part red, part glistening purple and looking impossibly bright in the relative darkness, "is forensic anthropological research?"

"From the fresh to the bloated, and finally the dry stage."

A clang sounded to the left. Seymour had moved to the nearby rusty car and stood wide-eyed looking inside the trunk. What could make the eyes of a forensic pathologist go that wide?

When Gray turned back, the glistening leg moved, and he jerked back and fell — hard, onto his behind and right onto a rock.

A While Before

Tomorrow, the headlines will read: The Stitcher's second victim met her doom at an isolated chalet in the woods.

I wait. I breathe, trying to hear the distant surf of British Columbia's Sunshine Coast, but it is too far away. The modern plastic chair feels hard. It's more the clamminess inside my leather jacket and pants, and the stink from the bowl of potpourri on the coffee table, which make me want to run out into the woods screaming.

Towering chalet windows overlook the darkened front drive where amorphous trees with moving limbs sway in the wind.

Lightning sparks in the sky, but in the reflection in the beaded glass I see startled eyes before they morph into big hollow crevices within a frightening contorted skull I scarcely recognize as mine.

My left hand trembles; I look down and steady it with the other. The insides of my leather gloves are already soaked, and I stare at the ski mask on my lap, loathe to put it on.

I don't want to kill. I'm not a killer.

Her car pulls up with a screech, headlights bleeding into the spitting rain. I yank the itchy mask over my face and try to even my jagged breathing.

Soon, she'll cover the path to the front door, so I grab my weapon from the table and rush across the room to a spot just left of the double doors.

I yank at the rope, ends now tightly wrapped around both fists, suddenly both excited and repelled. Is this really me?

Sweat drips down my forehead, stings my eyes, and I blink it away. Another flash of lightning and I catch my reflection again – this time, in mirrors covering the wall to the right of the doors. Damn.

My heart slams against my ribs. With another flash, she might see me before I strike, and then what? I imagine I hear the sound of steps on the paving stones outside.

She's coming.

I turn and whip up the carpeted stairs... her key engages the front door lock... a turning click. Rain slamming the overhead skylight is masking my rapid steps, and when the lightning inevitably flashes again, I'm upstairs on the railing.

I hazard a look down. She switches on a light which lengthens her distorted shadow directly below, while her rubber-soled shoes squeak against the shiny floor.

Panicked, I turn and pin my back against the hall wall – right next to her bedroom door – just as the sound of water flowing from the kitchen tap starts and stops, followed by the clink of glass against stone.

She's coming; she must be heading upstairs next.

I turn the knob and enter the small bedroom: I get my rope ready.

I've reached the point of no return, or perhaps passed it, who knows? After this, I'll never be the person I was: a good person; after this, I will be death. I wait behind the door.

It creaks open. She clicks on the light, and I am unprepared and blink.

I hesitate, and her face and shoulders turn towards me, the eyes a fraction ahead, widening at what they see. An arm moves up. Something glitters – I have to stop it – I have to stop it.

I wrap the rope around her neck and attack her from behind. She mouths the word 'no,' but I don't hear it. A drum pounds in my ears to the rhythmic beat of an African tribe ritual as I yank my fists together and twist... and twist.

It feels so good strangling her with that rope – even though my arm muscles burn – even though my insides are exploding... so powerful and glorious like I've never felt before. I'm the bringer of life and death – filled with a raging kind of blood – I am alive for the very first time.

She buckles under my grip.

I am no longer myself.

I am a killer.

CHAPTER TWO

GRAY STOOD AND pushed his heels into the ground, only just managing to avoid falling backward again. He was at the body farm and the glistening limb had moved. He shut his eyes. The air, thick and pungent, tasted of human flesh.

When he reopened his eyes, the blurred image of the leg came into focus.

Maggots swarmed across the rotting, open flesh of the calf, streamed down the ankle, and into the curdled ground.

He didn't have to continue with this case. Why not walk out of here without a backward glance, go on with his Christmas vacation? Sergeant Slope had jurisdiction.

Emmy came up beside him. "Are you alright, Chief Inspector?"

"I'm fine. It's the smell. I'm accustomed to one rotting body, two at most. A hundred is throwing me off."

"We currently have one hundred and eleven permanent residents."

"A kind of Hotel California," Gray said.

She blinked.

Seymour joined them. "Emmy hasn't told you the best part. Wait for it."

"What best part?" Gray said.

Emmy put her hands on her hips. Her red mouth looked coated in blood. "The lips, Chief Inspector. They were sutured shut, with 4.0 surgical nylon."

Both sets of eyes were upon him.

Seymour stepped closer. "Now, what do you make of that?"

Gray's world went blank.

"A surprisingly competent suturing job," Emmy said. "Although a 3.0 nylon is more cosmetically appropriate on the lips."

All sound… all thought flew into nothingness, before roaring back like a tidal wave crashing through Gray's head. Lips sutured, stitched? It couldn't be.

Not now—not here of all places, where his estranged wife and new-found two-year-old daughter lived.

Seymour stared at him, uncharacteristically quiet. He'd purposely left out the most pertinent detail, maybe because he couldn't bear to tell Gray, maybe because he knew you had to hook a fish before reeling him in.

Gray stepped closer to Emmy, his parched tongue stuck to the roof of his mouth. "Please repeat what you just said."

"Lips stitched with 4.0 nylon suture?" Emmy looked at Seymour and back and shrugged.

Did it not occur to her to mention the sutured lips sooner?

A steady rain beat his head, plastering down his hair, droplets flicking off the nearby tarp and pooling in one crinkled corner of the thick blue plastic. He grew so hot that the water going down his back felt like steam—and thoughts raced faster than he could reign in. Even as they sped out of control, a small voice told him to stop.

"You're shaking," Seymour said. "Breathe evenly."

But Seymour didn't understand the significance of what Emmy had revealed... the sutured mouth... the strangulation. Gray wasn't about to tell them.

"Dr. Kaur. We've been here for fifteen minutes, and you didn't bother to mention the sutured lips until now?"

Her eyes widened. "I explained in the order –"

"A maniacal killer strangles and mutilates defenseless women, evidence is being destroyed by the second, and you decided to explain things in order?"

"Easy, James. This isn't like you." Seymour moved between them. Gray pushed him aside.

"This... this isn't a very p-professional t-tone, Chief Inspector."

"I'm not the official officer-in-charge here. I don't need to be professional."

Gray frantically searched the grassed area for the one object he expected to find at the site—where was it? It wasn't there.

Seymour was muttering in a low tone. "I'm sorry about this, Emmy." He turned to Gray. "I'm sorry to you too, in a way."

"Don't trip over your remorse." In fifteen years on the force, he'd never lost control before; he'd never spoken this way to a witness before. What the hell had happened to him this past week? He controlled his voice. The words came out between clenched teeth. "That girl lay strangled, her lips sutured shut, murdered –"

Emmy stepped back. "But –"

"– and you're recounting your daily research routine."

"You don't understand –"

Seymour said, "Let her speak."

"You came back after making the call to the police from the cabin, didn't you?" Gray said.

"Y-yes, b-but, it isn't her –"

"And the body disappeared? How long did the call take?"

She lowered her head. "Four or five minutes."

"She's shutting down, James. Back off."

"Sergeant Slope d-didn't believe me," she said. "He said, no one dead."

"Slope accused her of making it up," Seymour explained. "He didn't understand Emmy any better than you, didn't understand her reactions, the way she sees the world."

Emmy blurted, "Neither of you understands. It isn't – her."

Gray pushed past Seymour. "Isn't who? Did you recognize the victim, is that what you mean? For God's sake, spit it out."

"I... I said... not her."

"Then who? Who was the dead girl?"

"Not a girl. Why did you think it was a girl? You misogynistic men are all the same. Always making sexist assumptions."

He caught Seymour's confused glance.

"The body I found wasn't a woman's. It belonged to a man. Now, do you understand? And then, someone took away the corpse. Slope didn't believe me. Do you?"

Gray took a deep breath and adjusted his perception of the crime scene. His brain began to work and sped forward. He scanned the area around the site for what he had expected to find. Two curious sets of eyes were upon him. He didn't plan on explaining.

He still couldn't find it. What the hell did that mean?

Five minutes later, they were back in Emmy's cabin.

The inside of her rustic house contrasted with the austerity of the body farm facility grounds.

Cedar lined the walls and soothed Gray's traumatized nostrils; an old sofa embroidered with flowers reminded him of his grandmother's cottage when he was a child; the heat from the roaring fire warmed his numb fingers and toes.

But his cramped right hand would take a while to recover, the three immobile middle fingers jutting forward like melting icicles, the scar snaking from wrist to forearm now red and raw.

It was a reminder of the most pivotal moment of Gray's life. An accident he may well have caused, which took everything, leaving only the nightly obsession to sculpt his son's face at age nine, ten, eleven – all the ages Craig would never see.

Gray had cut back on the obsession to sculpt. He fell asleep without the need now, a small success.

The color was returning to his stiff fingers, along with a burning sensation and pins and needles.

Gray returned to the present. "What your Emmy says – it isn't possible."

Seymour polished his glasses, fogged by the rain still pelting outside the cabin. "Yet, it is, my friend. We have to find this monster before he strikes again."

"You believe her? With no body and no evidence, I'm tempted not to."

Emmy sat on the dining table by the small open kitchen with her head lowered and her knees tightly together, a steaming mug between her hands. She seemed to be counting the ridges in the grain pattern of the worn oak table.

Her head lifted, and her face scrunched up, as though Gray were a particularly recalcitrant corpse who refused to decompose.

"There isn't much time," he said to Seymour. "We have to gather any possible evidence from the scene before the rain destroys everything. Minutes are vital."

Seymour shook his head. "Without SOCO?"

"Without a single scene of crime officer."

They left Emmy and headed back out towards site 144.

Rain pelted across his forehead and cheeks, tasted bitter in his mouth. The warmed wet clothes clinging to his body turned cold, making him shiver.

"You don't get Emmy, do you?" Seymour said.

"I can see that she struggles with social situations. She caught me off guard. I won't be as hard on her in the future."

They reached the site, and Gray lifted a corner of the blue tarp. Seymour took the other end, and as they together moved the six feet of plastic to one side, a gust of wind lifted it and spattered cold water from its surface onto their faces.

Gray blinked and pointed a few feet away.

"There. See those drag marks. They lead back towards the road." Marks that Slope might have seen earlier, before it rained, if he'd bothered to look.

The cramp in Gray's right hand worsened, along with the pins and needles. He clenched and unclenched his fist, trying to release the muscles.

"Why would Slope ignore these marks and disbelieve your witness?" Gray said.

"You don't know that he noticed them. Seems like an incompetent man to me."

"Not incompetent. More like self-serving. This town needs a sergeant."

Seymour rubbed his palms together and shuffled to keep warm. "Well the current holder of the sinecure seems like an obstinate ogre. You can thank Emmy for putting on the tarp, right? Admit it."

"I admit it. Although your friend doesn't know what she's dealing with, and neither do you."

The drag marks disappeared a few feet towards the center of the path as a slight downward incline caused the water to run

17

in a steady and muddy stream which pooled at one spot. No boot imprints or other marks were visible.

"Tell me more about Dr. Kaur," he said, sloshing towards the parking lot.

"Call her Emmy. She hates being called a doctor. Probably because clinical medicine never worked out for her."

Gray smiled. "The same applies to you. A dead patient has always been preferable to a live one, yet you make waiters refer to you by your title."

"To each their own."

Gray examined the ground. Dormant blueberry bushes looked like spiked skeletons awaiting their turn at glory.

"Something about this crime is making you react," Seymour said. "But what? You've solved countless grisly murders."

"Don't mess with a man with nothing left to lose."

"But you have something to lose now. That's what has splintered the calm you've achieved these last three years following the accident. You had nothing left to lose, so life became easy, uncomplicated. Enter Sita and Noelle. Your wife returns from a three-year absence, carting a toddler she never told you about, bringing risk – life beyond murder and death. Maybe you shouldn't have returned to Halfmoon."

Seymour invariably chose the most inopportune moments for his philosophical soliloquies. What could Gray say? Confiding never came naturally, and even if it had, he doubted he would say what he thought: that within him lay a solid and tranquil core capable of withstanding a hurricane; that he oscillated between Zen and obsession.

Seymour ran a hand through his wet hair. The widow's peak receded further back with each passing year, exposing a pink and flaky scalp.

18

Talking about the Stitcher suddenly became more difficult. Gray had to get that crazy image out of his mind.

"Who did you imagine lying there sutured when you lost control?" Seymour persisted. "It wasn't your wife. It was Noelle, wasn't it?"

Gray turned and resumed his search. Here, too, a steady stream of rainwater snaked across the ground towards the cottage. No other marks or evidence were visible. Seymour followed and kept talking.

"With only a few hundred people in this town, I can see why you'd be worried. But there's no indication we're dealing with a serial killer or one that targets children." He stopped Gray again. "Nothing's going to happen to Noelle."

"I won't inadvertently kill my daughter, you mean?"

Seymour paused.

Gray's breathing sounded heavy.

"You didn't kill your son," Seymour said.

"Sure I did." He didn't give the doctor a chance to reply. "I don't want details about the suturing leaking out to the public. It's imperative you grind that into Emmy. That kind of information stays within the investigation. I'll speak to Slope."

Seymour's long nose shadowed the thin albino-like lips. The expected retort never came.

They reached the narrow, winding dirt path leading out of the facility to the main road.

Seymour said: "Interesting name Sita chose: Noelle."

"All those years in Montreal, I never met a Noelle."

"Not one who was French, anyway. But the English like that name. I saw your ex-wife –"

"– we're not divorced."

"I know. I saw her with Slope the other day. Is that why you punched him?"

19

Who could resist punching that face? "We have a history," Gray said.

The torch light bobbed along the path, now muddy and flooded, until they reached the front gate from which they'd entered.

Stepping onto the gravel road, Gray flashed the torch onto a set of tracks heading up the mountain – the tracks he'd seen on their way in and mentioned to Seymour earlier.

"Look at these," he said running forward. "Those aren't from my car; we arrived from town, from the other direction. And your Emmy presumably drives that parked truck with the much wider tread. Now, who do you suppose these track marks belong to?"

"Slope's team? The last people who came to visit? I don't know; they could have been made at any time."

"Slope would have arrived from town, the way we did. These lead up the mountain. We need to ask your Emmy about any recent visitors."

The tracks disappeared within ten meters, washed away by the rain. If only they'd gotten to this evidence sooner instead of spending all that time talking.

A crunch sounded from the dense collection of cedars to the left. Was that a silhouette of someone standing about twenty feet away, shrouded by the branches, or was Gray imagining it? Before he could tell, the shadow was gone.

He sprang into action and ran. The cold air whipped his face. From behind, Seymour shouted his name – which would only serve to alert the culprit – which would only make it harder to catch The Stitcher.

Within seconds, he reached the spot, and despite the doctor's continued shouts to stop, to not risk going into the steep-edged thicket in the dark, Gray went in.

He shoved aside the tangled branches. Long, needle-like trunks faded into a globular darkness as he looked downward. Thorns scratched his face; the smell of black cottonwood and western red cedar filled his nostrils.

Immediately, he caught sight of the fleeing, amorphous shape. A rain-smudged ball of light bobbed down the jagged incline – moving towards the right fast and appearing and disappearing from within the trees – before disappearing around a large boulder.

Flashing his own light, Gray edged down the muddy mountainside – dead trunks and overturned branches making it a neck-breaking proposition. The BC forest could be deadly at night, even for the most experienced hiker. Around him, the call of timberwolves broke the background pitter-patter of the rain.

His feet descended the slope with a life of their own, anticipating debris, gripping the mulch and mud as well as his loafers could. Seymour had, at least, stopped shouting.

Gray reached the massive boulder. To its left, almost hidden in the dark, lay an unexpected near-vertical drop into a ravine.

Gray's foot slipped.

He caught himself by wrapping his arms around a maple, feeling its deeply-grooved bark scratch his face, smelling the musky, dense scent.

The lichen-coated rocks and ground slid under his feet, and it was all he could do to avoid slipping on the dead stumps jutting out of the ground, to move further from the ravine's edge before making his way to the boulder, and from there onto an incline that eventually led back towards the road.

Out here in the shrouded wilderness, only things immediately within the flashlight's beam remained visible.

Anyone might be lurking in the blackness – behind him, to his right or left – ready to push or stab or strike.

Gray decided to go straight ahead before climbing the incline back towards the road and Seymour.

Each crunching step was felt rather than heard over the sound of rain, the black oblivion to the left – probably only twenty feet down before curving back up the mountain – was a death trap nevertheless.

Gray stopped and switched off his torch. His breathing sounded heavy and loud; blood pounded through his ears.

A faint glimmer bobbed in the distance, so faint he barely saw it, but it left a fleeting impression on his retina in the otherwise pitch dark.

If he switched on the torch, he'd lose the distant glow. But without seeing where he stepped, something far worse could happen.

A hand touched his face, but it was only a clump of damp leaves from a bigleaf maple; their clammy surfaces slid across his cheek as he passed.

Deciding on compromise, he turned the torch on for a few paces, and then back off to identify the position of his target.

Of course, that meant the killer could track him, too.

This procedure led him about fifty feet away from the boulder, and now the distant torch shone from the top of the incline to Gray's right. The killer was making his way back towards the road.

Meaning what?

That the Stitcher was heading to a parked car? Or back to the farm and Emmy? Possibly meeting Seymour along the way?

Gray stepped up his pace to cover the distance between them.

Two green lights suddenly came towards him. He leapt back, nearly going over the edge of the embankment but instead catching himself on a tangled branch before hitting the ground.

Eyes – green and wild – lit up in his torch beam. An animal flew by him, narrowly missing his head and thumping down onto the muddy edge.

Another followed. Along with an ear piercing howl.

Wolves.

It could have been a bear. Up here, that was as likely as anything.

Best to get back to Seymour, quickly. The steep slope lay immediately to Gray's right.

Digging numb fingers into the dirt, he pulled himself up the forty-five-degree incline, feet sideways, the torch strap dangling from his mouth.

A foot at a time, he made his way up until a ledge appeared in the blackness, and the taste of dirt falling into his mouth was replaced by bile. Gray swallowed it down.

The road must be only a dozen meters or so ahead. The man Gray was chasing was likely out of reach, and any moment he would hear the sound of an engine starting, and the shriek of tires as the car raced away.

Now the distant rotting corpses felt as though they were close to his face, exuding a caustic scent. All those maggots and curdled flesh had seared his nostrils.

Something lurked in the darkness, eluding his grasp. The ledge was easy to climb, and ran about half way up the incline – until a punch sent him flying backward.

His feet slid out from under him, the world flipping, and the muddy slope at his face as black branches flew past and snapped… a trunk nearly within reach, but he missed it… and then something strong yanking his coat back. Stopping him from sliding.

"Got you!" Seymour said.

His dark head hovered over Gray, who now lay on the very edge of the ledge. "I wanted you to solve the case, James, not kill yourself in the process."

"Sorry to disappoint you." Gray's voice came out hoarse and cracked. He pushed himself up. "And thanks. Now I'm doubly glad I invited you to stay for Christmas."

"I don't know," Seymour said. "You wouldn't be in this mess if it weren't for me."

"Did you see him... or her?"

"I saw something whiz through the trees, but unlike you, I'm not brave enough to go chasing a demented killer in the dark."

Or Seymour was more concerned about finding his friend than catching the culprit. But Gray left that unsaid.

They climbed up to the road. Seymour panted as he tried to keep pace.

"What's the rush?" he said.

Gray had to know who that figure was, the identity of this Stitcher. He had to know right away.

"Okay, spit it out," Seymour said, now completely out of breath. "There's something you're not telling me."

His bony hand dug into Gray's arm, and they stopped. With the torch facing forward, Seymour's face lay shrouded in darkness, the pear-shaped outline of his large head backlit.

Overhead, the swaying pines danced to a tune Gray couldn't hear. For the first time, he felt excluded from his childhood haunt in these mountains, an innocence lost. But the rustling of the trees also reminded him of another time, another night such as this one – when a similar thing had happened.

24

"The Stitcher, John." His voice sounded low and foreign to his ears. He rarely used the doctor's first name, despite their growing friendship – perhaps because so many of their interactions revolved around cases, corpses, and crime scenes, perhaps to keep a professional distance. But he used Seymour's first name today. "That's what the press called the killer fifteen years ago. This scenario that Emmy described – strangulation, sutured lips – has occurred before. And the killer was never caught. Our quaint little community has a colorful crime history. If your Emmy is withholding information, her life could be in danger. I want to get back to the cabin, quickly."

Seymour looked down, his shadowed jowls tight and grim. An unnatural silence fell, as the rain suddenly ceased. Water glistened off Seymour's lashes under an emerging new moon peeking through spent clouds.

"You've been looking for something," the doctor said.

Was it safe to share that information with Seymour? Gray didn't answer.

"Could this be a copycat murder?" Seymour said, as they resumed their brisk walk.

Maybe, Gray thought – by an uninformed copycat who hadn't replicated the death precisely because they had no access to the original police file.

Seymour's moving profile looked pinched. "I assume you investigated this original Stitcher killing, fifteen years ago."

"I'm a cop. I was then, too, albeit a green one. We have to catch this killer, or there will be another victim, soon. I have to speak to your friend again, if she'll talk to me."

"Now that you're not yelling, I'm sure your Bond-like slickness will smooth the way."

They reached the cabin. All seemed quiet.

A wonderful warmth hit Gray when he entered the cabin, but within seconds, his soaked clothes felt like they were glued on.

He threw off his coat and noticed Emmy wiping down the tables and bookshelf – surfaces which looked like they hadn't seen a speck of dust in months.

Seymour rushed to her side. "Are you okay?"

"Yes, I'm fine." She lifted her chin.

"We'll find you a hotel."

"No. I can't leave the specimens."

"But –"

"No!" Her head turned towards Gray and then back to the bookshelf.

Gray kept his distance, but his instincts told him she had more to say. And he had to procure the information without a repeat of his earlier debacle.

Seymour held out his hands. "Emmy, we saw someone out by the road. He ran away, but the killer could return. How are you going to sleep here tonight?"

After some wavering, she faced Gray. Her body shook as she took two steps towards him.

"You won't get upset if I tell you something," she said.

"I'm sorry about earlier. I promise, I won't."

Emmy relaxed and let out a sigh. "Then I've remembered something else about the body, Chief Inspector. Something you should know, and something even the killer might not have noticed."

CHAPTER THREE

IT STARED BACK at her from her pubis.

The unbelievable nerve!

Her electric razor had shorn a path across her thigh, chomping like an inadequate lawn mower over dry summer grass before reaching her bikini line – and there it was: smack in the middle.

A solitary gray hair.

Farrah Stone saw red.

How could this happen to her? Other people yes, but not her.

Turning forty-five wasn't for the faint-hearted, not when looks had once been a currency which now threatened to become defunct. She might still pass for thirty-five – on a well-rested day – but for how bloody long?

Outside, a few rays penetrated the inveterate winter sky. She kept her bathroom extra hot, not quite a dry sauna but close – if only to protect her from the bone-chilling dampness omnipresent on the West Coast, where clouds became trapped between mountains and spat on her on a regular basis.

Salty air leaking through a crack in the window touched her nostrils and mingled with her guava infused body lotion, rose hand cream, and her multitude of bath oils.

This upcoming Christmas Eve, on her birthday, she would have officially outlived her father.

Her father had never given her a present for either Christmas or her birthday, and his love hadn't grown from the day she was born to the moment of his death. But he had left her the one thing she valued the most. And she would always cherish it.

Farrah's mother, on the other hand, was a closed book, best left closed.

That both her parents had keeled over during their morning runs (on separate mornings) was also something not to be contemplated in depth.

She reflected on this superficially and unemotionally, thinking she'd sidestepped her parents' atherosclerosis by virtue of regular fasting and exercise; every subsequent moment that she would outlive her father's forty-five years highlighted how she had won.

Farrah finished shaving. Then she smoothed a palm-full of lemon scented lotion over each slim leg in long, slow caresses. Cool lotion over hot skin. Sensation. The feeling of being alive – it gave her life meaning and purpose.

It also made her think of Gray James, who was back at Halfmoon Bay for Christmas – the dark, contained type you'd eagerly open your legs for, and not kick out of bed afterward.

It made her think of sex and the visceral, full-body reaction she'd experienced when she saw him last week. Those striking emerald eyes of his looked intense enough to see through her clothes. The black hair, cut to perfection, would feel great between her fingers. Incredible as it grazed the insides of her thighs –

Farrah opened her legs, spread the lotion upward. So sexy, that deep baritone voice –

A clanging ringtone from her cell made her start.

Teddy had given it to her as an early birthday present, and she hadn't had time to change the ringtone to something more Zen. Perhaps she'd choose the trickle of raindrops, or a faint monastery bell.

Amazing how so small a detail highlighted their inherent incompatibility. But Theodore Roland Atkins, self-proclaimed squire of the village, magnanimous to everyone, most especially himself, wasn't the one calling her.

She put away the razor and carried the phone into her bedroom. The caller's voice mingled with the sound of footsteps shuffling outside her door.

"What are you saying?" Farrah hissed into the phone. "No! That's nonsense. Now, stop calling me."

She hung up; her pulse beat fast. Donning her gold-trimmed, satin robe, she pulled the collar tight across her neck. "Who's there? Why are you hovering outside my room?"

Matisse opened the door but didn't meet her eyes. His birth name had been Samuel, but she'd quite rightly changed it.

Her shoulders relaxed. Nobody had heard the call – only her adopted son.

"Come and help me brush my hair, will you?" She reached for her pearl choker, latched it on, and sat before the vanity.

His lanky form shuffled towards her in the mirror, hunched, the multitude of white-tipped pimples on his forehead, nose, and cheeks practically popping out of his face, reminding her of miniature volcanoes.

Sighing, she shook her head; he paused mid-step. He was so sensitive, always watching her every gesture and expression for signs of reassurance and approval, almost as though he needed her blessing to exist.

How exhausting. Thank goodness Farrah had never exposed her father to that selfishness. He had always compared her beauty to the reclining white stone sculptures at his gallery – faceless, nude, and cold. 'All art is life,' he'd tell her, believing himself to be a connoisseur of both.

On this milestone birthday, a realization came to mind: any casual approach to life got you to forty-five; but afterward, each person awoke alone in the morning, struggled in the deep end of a pool, flailing, ready to grab whichever lifeline could keep depression and age at bay. Who she was inside would begin to show.

Matisse came closer and stood behind her, smelling of chewing gum and wafting foot odor.

He reached for her silver-handled brush and began a hundred strokes she'd taught him when he'd first arrived thirteen years earlier. She closed her eyes and held back her head. The bristles massaged her scalp.

"Mom, can I speak to you about something?"

"Hmm?" Farrah replied. The brush skimmed her forehead and moved down inch by inch. She felt bathed in sensation.

"It's about Delilah."

That yanked her out of the moment, and she whipped her head around. The boy ruined everything. She hated acknowledging Teddy's daughter, much less talking about her.

"What about Delilah?"

Matisse's oval and chinless face bore down on her; he chewed the gum like a cow.

"I kinda like her," he said. "Is that okay? I mean, since you're gonna marry her dad, and we'd become brother and sister. But we aren't really related, and with both of us adopted there aren't any blood ties."

He waited, expecting something, always hoping. Delilah hooking up with Matisse? That vibrant, and let's be honest, slutty skank associating with Farrah's pathetic boy?

She didn't mask her lopsided smile. Turning towards the mirror, she said: "You and Delilah? You think she'd want you?"

He had fastened the top button of his shirt. "Pull out that shirt, Matisse. How many times do I have to tell you not to tuck?"

His face grew red; he stiffened and stopped chewing. The miniature volcanoes on his nose threatened to erupt, and she pulled back.

Sometimes, she scarcely recognized him as the boy she'd brought home. Sometimes, he took the form of a stranger who didn't like her, didn't love her. No one loved her.

Farrah forced herself to relax.

He was only a child under that grown body – in need of a mother, and she'd been harsh. She of all people should know that any affection stroked a child's soul, even artificial affection.

What did love feel like? She'd read about it studying liberal arts at UBC, a lifetime ago. She'd awaited its embrace all these years, but it had yet to come.

"I'm sorry," Farrah said, reaching for his hand. It was warm and clammy, but she hid her cringe. That's what mothering was. Concealing your real feelings for the benefit of your child.

She caressed his hand, and this seemed to help. His slumped posture returned, the lower full lip quivered. Empty pools of wanting stared at her from behind his square-rimmed glasses. So needy.

"You don't believe me and Delilah belong together?" he said.

"I didn't say that, Darling. It isn't what I believe that matters. What does she have to say?" Farrah felt proud of her response. Any mothering site would approve.

He shuffled toward the door. Good, he'd leave soon. The discussion was becoming tedious.

"She hasn't said anything."

"But you've told her how you feel?"

"She doesn't know," he said.

Farrah smiled again, this time concealing the smile under her hand.

He seemed reluctant to leave. Farrah picked up a pencil and expertly applied liner to her eyes, her hands as steady as when she'd worked as a makeup artist in the Vancouver film industry – years ago, before she'd taken over her father's art gallery.

"Delilah's going out with Sergeant Slope," Matisse said. "Teddy knows about it, and he's fuming."

Perhaps it was for the best. Why not have Theodore Atkinson's fake blue blood mix with the common local constabulary? She could see no loss to herself. It might even provide some amusing anecdotes to supply to her future house guests – at Teddy's expense.

Yes, always at Teddy's expense. And in more ways than one.

Matisse hesitated at the door. "Who just called? You sounded upset, maybe even scared."

Should she tell him? No, not yet. "No one. Everything's fine."

He looked unconvinced as he left.

Farah resumed the strokes before firmly putting down her brush.

She considered resuming something else, but Gray James's delicious face wouldn't come clearly to her mind; besides, Matisse had wrecked her mood.

That only left one thing to take care of before all else.

No way would she leave the offending thing in place.

Moving to the bathroom, she found her tweezers inside an ivory storage box, peeled open the gold satin robe, and spread her legs.

Violently, she yanked the offending gray hair out.

.

CHAPTER FOUR

"A STORM'S COMIN' in a couple of days, folks."

The weatherman's voice boomed over the car radio.

Gray car curved along Redrooffs Road (named after a resort which once featured red roofs) and turned onto Mintie before parking alongside the public beach.

As a small community of about 2,800 people, many of whom were summer residents, Halfmoon Bay was among the quieter of the Sunshine Coast towns. It had an elementary school, but the locals attended high school in nearby Sechelt or Gibson.

Residents also shopped or visited their favorite restaurant chains in Sechelt since Halfmoon had only a general store, a bistro/café, and a spa and meditation center. It functioned as a quiet tourist destination for those who fancied hiking, kayaking, sailing, or a couple of romantic nights in rustically furnished beachside resort tents.

Gray sat in the car facing the scalloped bay, protected from the sea by South Thormanby Island and Vancouver Island. He'd once taken a sailboat beyond this protective cove. Things had never been the same again.

"Get ready to latch up your windows and pile the sandbags," the voice over the radio said.

Mintie Road glistened, resembling a picture postcard. Lights highlighted the wooden pier, customers bustled around inside Sammy's General Store, and the beautiful smell of coffee and croissants drifted outward from My Alibi, the bistro/café. The restaurant was a piece of Montreal transported to the West Coast, obsessed with all things French, as was the owner.

Gray took a moment before tackling the unpleasant ordeal ahead. A walk up the short pier would clear his head. Not only was he about to meet with Sergeant Slope, but the location meant seeing someone else.

The slate-colored water rose in white-tipped peaks and crashed upon the pebbly beach to his left. A cold spray moistened his cheeks, carrying a salty seaweed tanginess. Was it his imagination or did the tree-covered islands in the distance resemble sleeping animals, ready to awaken and jump up at any moment?

A pleasant calm filled him – a solitary calm – and time, beauty, and nature stood still. Bringing forth a familiar peace. This place had been one of his homes as a child; he had roots here. He would deal with whatever challenges lay ahead.

Multiple bright purple starfish, known as ochre sea stars, hid between the rocks near the shoreline. Their numbers had recovered after the 2016 viral epidemic which had 'melted' nearly forty-percent of the sea star population. They helped to brighten the scene before him, inciting a hint of what Gray had felt while standing on this pier in his youth. That young man remained a part of him, still.

He left the pier and made his way to My Alibi, prepared to face the music.

Inside, the mingled scents of pastry, meat, and coffee brought back memories of Montreal. And he felt a little homesick for the stylish yet slinky summer dresses; the restaurants bustling with business even on a frigid Tuesday night; the historic French architecture.

Sergeant Slope sat at a center table, looking like he owned the place. Slope, with his ski-slope nose and heavy-lidded eyes which followed you around, unblinking.

Gray would have preferred to have their informal talk in a more private setting, but Slope had insisted. It wasn't hard to guess why.

A bump betrayed a blue and purple bruise on Slope's chin, expertly covered up with makeup. Who had applied the makeup, Gray wondered.

"What about your vacation, Chief Inspector?" Slope said bringing a fork to his mouth. He had already ordered and held a perfectly square piece of coq monsieur on a fork, inches from his thin, pink lips. Who cut a ham and cheese sandwich?

Gray sat on the retro, trendy-torn chair opposite. Large acrylics and oils, all for sale and by local BC artists, covered the walls. Overhead, Blondie sang about how she would get you.

"This is your case, Reggie, not mine."

"Now isn't that sweet of you to say. Cheeky even, given what's gone on between us. But you're wasting time. Emerald Kaur's off her rocker."

Gray leaned back; the chair creaked. Hopefully, it wouldn't break under him. "Why don't you believe Dr. Kaur?"

"A better question might be, why do you? With no actual body, and no report of a missing person. And here, of all places, in our quiet little village."

He gestured towards the window. It overlooked the amoebic arms of land on either side of the bay, the elevated terrain dotted with rustic, colorful cottages overlooking the seascape. A blue-and-white awning covered the outdoor patio – functional and used by hearty British Columbia residents all year long. Canadians were accustomed to sitting outside in their winter coats while cradling a coffee between cold hands. Gray was surprised to see the ice-cream counter closed.

"Dr. Kaur's a lonely weirdo who most of the women around here can't stand and would kick out of town if they could," Slope said. "Now, me – I take things slowly, get to know my neighbors before casting judgment."

"And?"

"It's hard to trust any person who won't look you in the eye. That body farm doesn't bother me, Sir." He stressed the 'Sir' with a lift of one eyebrow. "Maybe it should."

"Does it bother others?"

Slope's chuckle made chewed food trickle out of his mouth and onto his lower lip. He licked it back with a snake-like tongue.

"You don't know the half of it. She's got fifty body donations at the farm with eighty more planned. Imagine that. Now, she wants to expand, but the town's fightin' it. Bodies bring smell, vultures circlin' around our town. Not to mention the ghoulish reputation which doesn't do tourism any good. And our local bigwig Teddy Atkinson is funding all this alleged research. It's his land, not the university's, and it ain't hers either. I wouldn't be surprised if things between Dr. Kaur and the town folk don't explode – especially the women town folk."

"Why them in particular? And what does that have to do with you believing her about the murder? Reggie, the body Emmy found was mutilated."

"You mean he had his lips sewn up like a purse? Like in the old murder case my boss handled. He told me all about it."

"Did he?" Gray said. "You must remember how complicated things became in this town."

Slope's brow relaxed. He sat back and crossed his arms over his poorly pressed shirt. A portion of the collar looked scorched. Noticing Gray's gaze, the other man's eyes narrowed over Gray's immaculate maroon silk shirt.

"Yes, I served under Inspector Ray at the tail end of that case," Slope said. "It was exactly like this made-up account. Sutured lips but nothing left at the scene. We never found the guy, but that's neither here nor there."

"Why?" Gray couldn't believe it. Slope seemed to be breaking every investigative rule. Every protocol for keeping the public safe – and it made no sense.

But the sergeant was enjoying making him wait for a response; he knew something Gray didn't. Something which excused ignoring a grotesque crime and letting evidence wash away with yesterday's rain, not to mention risking the return of the town's most infamous killer.

Slope's half-smile and unblinking stare grated. Watching the man chew wasn't much fun either.

"Because of the first bogus report," Slope finally said. "Of a girl with her mouth sewn shut."

"First report? What first report?"

But they were interrupted.

A tanned hand, the sight of which made an elastic band snap in Gray's chest, reached over and placed a bowl and a pastry before him. A maple and pecan scone sat in place of the usual croissant. They must have just come out of the oven.

He looked up; his wife's chocolate brown eyes met his.

"I didn't need to ask what you wanted," Sita said.

That bond of familiarity – from knowing someone for years, living with them day in and day out, could sometimes break. In their case, it had, and it hadn't.

Gray tried not to think about it and instead lifted the French-inspired bowl of café au lait with two hands and drank, closing his eyes for a moment.

That first sip of coffee was always his favorite moment of the day. A ritual which civilized an uncivilized world – the nutty scent, the astringent and slightly sour taste.

And Sita had a gift for all things culinary, making her purchase of My Alibi a perfect career fit.

"That's a friggin big coffee," Slope said.

"Gray likes to think he's French," she replied, facing the sergeant. She and Slope shared the mutual smile longer than strictly necessary.

"How's Noelle?" Gray asked Sita.

"Perfect. I'll bring her over to your Dad's later."

She moved to the next customer and took some of the room's warmth with her. Slope's youthful yet calculating eyes followed. With everything going on, Gray needed this complication about as much as a hole in the head.

He shoved his personal feelings aside and leaned across the table. "What first bogus report?"

The sergeant began cutting another perfect square of his sandwich with his knife and fork.

"Of a girl with her lips sutured," he said. "About a month ago. A kid found the body in the family back yard, or so he said, but he's been known to lie lots of times. I went there and – nothing. If you ask me, our crazy doctor heard about it and is making this latest event up."

"Why?"

"Who knows why crazy women do what they do?"

Grays pulse drummed in his ears. He'd never liked this man, and this interaction slammed more nails into that coffin.

39

Why had Sita given Slope that long, almost affectionate look? How might this affect his budding father-daughter relationship with Noelle? A second chance at being "Daddy."

Coming home for Christmas to where the accident had happened had thrown Gray into a deep and dark hole. He was poised hanging from the edge with one hand – and not his good one.

There was always another step to climb up on the metaphorical ladder. Life made certain of that. But how could he learn to live with both realities: not caring what happens, and needing to care?

The scone was buttery and perfect, leaving the requisite number of crumbs on his lap.

"Did this child – the one who found the first body – recognize the victim?" Gray asked.

"Alleged body, Chief Inspector. Yeah, he said it was his babysitter. A young girl by the name of Joanie Skolowski. But I know the kid was lyin'."

"How do you know?"

"The family got an email from Joanie, after the kid allegedly saw her body. They forwarded the email to me.

"Do you mind if I see it?" Gray asked, keeping his tone even. "As a professional courtesy. It's your case, of course."

The other man was being bloody courteous given how he felt about Gray – yet that was Slope: calculating and inhuman in a way Gray could recognize but never understand. He felt a familiar pang of concern for his estranged wife.

For three years, she'd fallen off the face of the Earth. And he recalled, again, the sway of her hips as she walked away on that Montreal beach – not blaming him, but not able to look at him either.

Slope shrugged in response to Gray's request.

"Now why should I? As you say, this isn't your case."

"You need to get SOCO to the site."

The other man nearly choked. "Out here? They gotta come from Gibsons. Might as well call in the RCMP if I'm gonna have egg on my face. I can't justify that with no corpse to cut up."

Seymour had accompanied Gray to the Vancouver police department on a temporary exchange program.

"I have a top-notch forensic pathologist staying with me. He can at least go over the scene officially." Gray didn't add that Seymour had already done so – unofficially.

"Hey," Slope said, chewing. "I get that you need to keep busy. I hear you're havin' trouble with the time off."

Did the whole damn village know his personal business? Dad must be gossiping with the locals, but despite only having spent summers here during his youth, the village residents saw Gray as one of their own and not as the Chief Inspector with an impeccable record for solving murders.

He was just 'Gray' to them. To some: poor, unfortunate man; to others: that bastard who deserved what he got. He much preferred the latter.

Donning his poker face, Gray watched Sita chatting happily while taking another customer's order two tables over. It was like watching a stranger he'd spent ten years with move about the room.

So far, Slope had been running this discussion; Gray had allowed it. The time had arrived to apply a subtle change of course.

"Now that you have a second report of a mutilated victim, shouldn't you investigate this further? On the off chance this isn't a hoax. I don't know how you'll justify another death to your superiors."

41

Slope put down his cutlery. "Especially after some big shot chief inspector from Vancouver offered to help? Or are you just in BC for a bit, before you head back to Montreal?"

Gray drank his latte and put the bowl down. "That isn't decided, yet."

The other man pursed his thin lips. "I guess I'd better cooperate with you, then."

"Like you always do."

Slope glared back. If he wanted a fight – personal or professional – he'd get one.

The shrill ring from Slope's phone broke the silent showdown.

"What?" the sergeant said to the caller. "Where is it?" He listened to the person on the other end. "I'll be there as soon as I can. Tell them to keep their shirts on." Looking up at Gray, he added, "I'm bringing someone with me."

Slope hung up and stared unblinkingly. "Gotta check something out. I guess you're my shadow until we go back to the farm."

"We should pay for our food," Gray said, standing and straightening his abused back. He wished Sita would switch to comfortable, non-hipster chairs which were less than fifty years old. Did everything from his childhood warrant a trendy comeback?

"I don't pay for my food here," Slope replied, wearing a smile so smug that Gray's working fist clenched.

Outside, cold rain slashed diagonally across the country road and adjacent bay, and a gust nearly toppled Gray. The muddy grass sank under his boots.

He reached his car, parked across from Slope's SUV. "Where are we going?"

Slope yelled through the wind. "Blow Hole Cove. Which goes up and down a mountain range; pretty bumpy and rocky. We'll take my wheels."

The inside of Slope's truck smelled of leather, cigarettes, and damp. The sergeant's hair framed a long face, and small ears made all the more noticeable by the apostrophe-shaped sideburns. Elvis would have approved.

During the bumpy ride, Gray kept his eyes on the distant snow-topped mountains which stood majestically, rimmed with a thin mist. Wipers sliced back and forth across the windshield, screeching like a bird.

"That storm's coming sooner than they think," Gray said.

"Naw. It's like this every winter by the coast. It'll blow over in minutes. You've been gone a long time; you forgot."

Slope's feminine hands gripped the steering, betraying a tension otherwise concealed. Light reflected off his hand. The square gold base on his ring finger had a center diamond.

Which made Gray recall the vital evidence Emmy had delivered upon their return to her cabin last night – after Gray had unsuccessfully chased the killer.

Evidence that had perhaps slipped by the Stitcher.

Should Slope be on Gray's list of possible suspects? That seemed impossible... and yet...

Blow Hole Cove came into view as they came out from behind a cluster of pine and descended a winding road. The rain had eased, but the wind still packed a punch, jolting the truck back and forth.

Gray could imagine his Lotus skidding off the wet road, flying through the air, and flying off the cliff edge to the left and into the bubbling sea.

There were many coves in the area, but this one was the hardest to reach.

Ahead, a thirty-foot yacht became visible and swayed on the white-peaked waves close to the adjacent rocks. Far too close. The tan sail rippled and jerked.

Slope pulled up to the cove and parked at one side of the gravel parking lot. "These guys say they've got engine trouble. Otherwise, all boats gotta be docked in Buccaneer Marina."

"That's not far; they can make it, even in those waters."

"They'd better."

Gray stepped out of the truck onto surf-worn pebbles of maroon, pewter, and black.

Two men and a woman, floating figures in the mist, stood on the deck.

Gray's blood went cold.

One of the men stepped off the boat and met Slope, gesturing with his burly hand, scrunching his sea-weathered face. The other leaned against the rail on the deck.

The woman had already slipped inside – but not before giving Gray a split second to catch her profile. Not before giving Gray a chance to see who she was.

He froze; the wind whipped across his face and body, fluttering the open ends of his jacket.

How could she be here of all places?

What was going on in this town?

CHAPTER FIVE

WHAT WOULD A STORM do to her forensic specimens?

Too many issues vied for Emmy's attention, attacking her, almost stinging the surface of her skin in a hundred imagined bites.

This facility was her life. Looking through her cabin's kitchen window at the silently threatening clouds overhead, she knew a storm was coming.

What should she do with her residents? Leave them to the elements or move the bodies to the secure steel shed constructed for just such a purpose?

Teddy's estate manager, Butch, could help, but displacing the bodies would contaminate the project findings. Not to mention the harm Butch and his brutes would undoubtedly inflict. She'd have to report the displacement in her study conclusions, and any results would become immediately suspect. And she'd have to talk to Butch. She hated talking to Butch.

A less severe storm could add to the authenticity of the research. Part of her directive involved documenting the effects of incremental weather on human remains.

But that hardly extended to having a flood sweep the bodies from their respective sites and lodge them amongst dense bush and pine for miles around. She couldn't do that to her residents — people who had entrusted their remains to her research.

Would the University of British Columbia ever fund her again if months of data were destroyed? Beyond supporting herself financially, how would she fill her empty days without having specimens to check, monitor, and evaluate? They were her family in a way. God help her, they were.

She punched in Butch's number. His low, grating "Yeah?" made her cringe. She could imagine his hollow, soulless eyes staring ahead as he spoke.

"It's time," she said. Teddy had already apprised him of the situation.

"Humph."

With that elegant retort, he hung up. He and his men would be coming.

She breathed, relieved to be alone at the moment. Solitude felt simpler than the alternative. Always. But that was part of her high-functioning autism, which had been diagnosed late – partly because most research had been done on boys; partly because shy and withdrawn behavior was often dismissed in girls.

Emmy had never been disruptive or drawn to technology or math. But at age twelve, she'd become obsessed with the retro *Charlies Angels* TV show, collecting all the posters, promotional cards, and stickers she could find of Kelly, her favorite. She'd also hidden under the wing of one girl or other at school.

It wasn't until adulthood that Emmy had faced another symptom: her hypersexuality. And stamped it down.

The overhead sky seemed low enough to reach.

Best to get some of the lighter things done before Butch's arrival. Some of the isolated limbs and arms were delicate, and she could more safely manage them on her own.

Outside, the wind slapped her face, and she brought together the collars of her jacket. The decomposition wafted over more strongly than on regular days. Today, the smell bothered even her, as though another pungent scent — something far more malignant than mere death — had mingled with and supervened the usual order.

She strode over to the shed, yanked the door open, retrieved the necessary rope, and slammed it shut. Hard.

The loneliness which had compelled her to work all through Christmas had quadrupled since she found the murdered man. Now more people would attack her; more people would hate her.

She wound the rope around one of the bins; secured it to the adjacent maple. The car would survive any gale; still, the rusty lock on the trunk might give way. But the exposed corpses presented a far more significant problem.

Tires crunched over gravel nearby. So quickly?

Butch came towards her in a simian stride, his long coat rustling in the wind. She didn't make eye contact. Those black irises of his reflected a deadness her residents didn't possess. Another man followed him, thinner, less threatening.

"What needs doing?" Butch said.

"The specimens in the car, coffins, and the buried bodies are likely fine. Although we should tie up the car, so the lock doesn't snap open in the wind. We need to secure the remaining bins against the wind and any flood, and the free-lying bodies need covering."

His frown deepened; every muscle in his thickset body threatened to pounce on her without warning as he shouted over the wind. "Not movin'?"

"Only one or two. For the rest, let's nail down the special weatherproof covers. You'll find them stored in the shed for

47

just such an occasion. Any other questions before we proceed?"

He hesitated, looked towards the dense, swaying pine and Douglas fir, and then at her.

"Mr. Atkins wants to know if you'll consider stayin' at the big house. He's worried."

Emmy nearly tripped over her tongue. "Yes! I'd love to."

She'd spent most of last night drifting in and out of a hazy nightmare in which a severed hand hovered overhead, wielding a suture needle.

After she'd refused the offer of a motel room, Dr. Seymour had asked her to stay at the Chief Inspector's cottage, but she'd never share a roof with him. No matter how much terror she felt.

Butch continued to shout over the wind. "Boss says, you may as well come to the party, too."

His tone suggested she ought to refuse, that she shouldn't be allowed to socialize with Teddy Atkinson and his anorexic companion Farrah Stone. What right did this Neanderthal have to judge her?

The two men did their work, moving the more fragile bodies to the shed and securing the others.

Butch surveyed the job and turned to face her. The deep crevices from his nose to his mouth and the pitted skin on his cheeks made him appear older than his forty or so years. He spat out the words.

"The party – it's gonna be fancy."

"Teddy invited me."

"Pine Cove Mansion ain't no place for half-breeds."

Emmy stood, dumbfounded.

How long had it been since someone called her that? But the childhood insult stung a thousand-fold more now – in this place, delivered by this man. The hundred imagined bites suddenly morphed into a thousand.

Approaching voices interrupted her retort. The wind must have drowned any sound from the cars entering the parking lot.

Now, figures emerged from around the bend. A dozen or so women carrying banners and sticks, and wearing surgical masks marched in her direction. Some of them looked familiar; others must be from surrounding towns.

Emmy swallowed. The masks reminded her of the suturing, the spread-eagled corpse, and all the horrific events of the last twenty-four hours.

She took a step back before stopping, deciding to hold her ground. They had no right to be on her turf, whoever they were.

Farrah Stone strode front and center, chin down, eyes pinned on Emmy.

The other women, her 'Angels' as some of the townspeople joked, followed her like rabbits, invariably supporting whatever cause Farrah had torn off with her teeth.

Unfortunately, Farrah's latest mission involved boycotting and shutting down the body farm and convincing her fiancé Teddy to withhold its funding.

The various banners read: *No Dead Bodies; Kill the Body Farm; Stop the Vulture.*

Emmy marched towards the women on wobbly legs that weren't her own. Her voice cracked. "What are you doing here? This is a research facility and private property. Get out now."

"We don't want you near our towns," Farrah said, removing her mask. "Look at those vultures." A single scavenger circled overhead. "They chew up your bodies and spit them out on our playgrounds. It's disgusting, and so are you."

The Farm was twenty minutes from any residential development. Farrah's face didn't look distressed; if anything

— Emmy tried... tried hard to read that expression — the horrible woman looked pleased.

"I'm raising my daughter here," another woman said. "We can't have chunks of corpses rotting in our backyards."

Despite the mask, Emmy recognized her as Sita, the owner of a bistro in the village. Seymour had mentioned something about her and Chief Inspector James being estranged husband and wife.

"You shouldn't be doing this kind of work," Sita said. "It's indecent."

How much more remote could Emmy get than two hours away from Vancouver? These uneducated Barbies didn't understand medical work, research, the need to be within commuting distance of a university.

It was hard to know how to respond. "Get out, all of you. I-I'm calling the police."

Farrah stepped forward. "Go ahead. Slope's in the palm of my hand, and everyone knows it. He won't arrest us, won't stop us if we set your body farm on fire. That's what these poor corpses need, by the way, a good cremation. You should pray you don't burn with them."

Sita's head jerked up. Perhaps Farrah had gone too far for comfort.

Emmy moved her feet apart and pushed her heels into the ground. "Teddy owns this land. Not you."

"Is that what you think? When we're married, you won't have a sandbox to dig in, let alone acres of prime BC land."

Where was Butch in all this? Emmy scanned the area and saw his receding figure in the distance. He apparently didn't wish to alienate his boss's future wife. Meanwhile, a couple of the women approached nearby specimens. One kicked a limb encased in plastic.

"Stop that." Emmy ran forward, causing the other woman to jump back before Emmy tackled her to the ground. The resultant scream bled through the air.

The police had to be called. The woman on the ground continued screaming.

Scrambling to her feet, Emmy made for the cabin, zig-zagging around protestors attempting to tackle her along the way.

She reached the front door before them, swung it open, and ducked inside – slamming it in time to shut the closest woman out.

She turned the bolt. Pounding sounded on the door, and it shook on its hinges. Would they break it down? Were they damaging her specimens this very moment?

After punching 911, she spoke fast, shouting at dispatch to send the police, impatiently blurting out the words because she needed to get back quickly before they did more damage.

An axe leaned against the corner wall. They were attempting to frighten her. She would not be frightened.

The door opened with its characteristic squeak. The wind whipped through her hair as she confronted the semicircle of glaring residents determined to drive her out of town.

Farrah and Sita had joined them.

Emmy stepped forward, widened her stance, and held the axe positioned to strike.

"Move back, ladies. Or else..."

All the women moved back.

"Anyone who touches a specimen," Emmy yelled, "is going to become part of this farm. Do you understand?"

The showdown began.

CHAPTER SIX

RECOGNITION STRUCK GRAY first, followed by surprise. Two men and a woman were on the boat.

She was here, of all places? Not in Montreal where he'd last seen her. Something must have made her leave home and the safety of the department.

The thirty-foot yacht rocked back and forth, docked in the water on Blow Hole Cove, with the name *"The Isabelle"* printed on one end.

The cove lived up to its name. As Gray approached, seawater burst upward from a hole in the rocks, letting out a whooshing sound. As he understood it, sea caves grew landwards and upwards into vertical shafts and exposed themselves to the surface to form a blow hole. And intermittently, water under hydraulic pressure pumped up and out, fifteen feet into the air.

Smooth pebbles rolled and crunched under his boots, and the tangy sea-scent wafted into his nostrils as he watched Slope approach the man who had left the boat. The other sailor, burly and hirsute, leaned against the rail, staring.

Slope looked his way, just as the woman on the boat disappeared inside — but not before she'd allowed Gray to recognize her.

A protective urge leaped inside him, but he had no intention of sharing this fact with the sergeant, who glanced from Gray to the deck, a question in his eyes, before resuming his discussion with the boat's captain.

"You gotta take this yacht back out," Slope said.

"No can do," the other man said. "We have trouble with the engine, see. And even without that, there's no way my crew can handle these waters. We're stuck here, Sergeant. Face it."

The wind blew back the captain's wiry hair, revealing a robust and horizontal brow. His cracked red lips formed a snarl.

As if on cue, a wave jerked the boat up, nearly crashing it onto the rocks. What was she doing on the thing? She had to get off, now.

An experienced sailor could navigate the boat to safety, even in this weather. Gray himself could manage it — if he ever planned on boarding a yacht again in his life – which he didn't.

He ran a rough hand through his hair, turned, and moved towards the towering wall of granitic rock at the edge of the cove.

After about fifteen feet, Gray passed the narrow entrance to one of the caves on his left. The putrid scent of bat droppings emanating from inside made him turn the other way, and head back to the others.

She didn't want to be identified, or else she wouldn't have gone below deck. She didn't want him to say anything.

That briefly afforded glimpse of her profile — it must have been to allow him time to understand, to withhold any reaction. How often had she held his life in her hands, and vice versa? Trust reigned between them, as did friendship.

"I'll get my engineer out here," the captain bellowed. She'll tell you; the boat needs repairs."

He yelled for someone named Chloe.

Gray covered the remaining distance back to the boat in a sprint.

He suspected that soon, he'd be walking away, leaving her with them, not knowing why. Even as a figure stepped out of the cabin – a dark, feminine form with short brown hair – he disciplined himself not to speak, not to act.

Detective Vivienne Caron, his second-in-command during his years in Montreal, didn't look at him. She rubbed grease off her long-fingered hands with a dirty cloth and addressed the captain.

"Yes?"

Her musical French intonation, characteristic of certain Québecois, suddenly made him feel homesick.

"Tell him about the engine," the captain said.

"I'm having trouble with the generator," she said. Her eyes flicked Gray's way, so briefly only he must have noticed.

Her face was serene; no bruises, no anxiety. Vivienne was more than capable of taking care of herself. Still — out at sea with these two unsavoury characters, who know what could happen? She'd had personal troubles at home; he'd contributed to them in a way, but this? What would make her leave her job and come to the West Coast?

"I can't guarantee we won't break down somewhere in the water," she said to Slope. The captain lifted his chin and smiled.

With the yacht disabled, Vivienne would at least remain on solid ground. The second man continued to lean against the rail and silently chewed his gum, the horizontal ridges running deep across his forehead. Thick tufts of hair grew on his forearms.

Slope instructed them to make the repairs quickly, while Vivienne returned below deck.

Any explanation would have to wait until she contacted him — but he wouldn't like it. Whatever she'd been through back home, working undercover and infiltrating these ruffians wasn't her style.

Slope kept pace beside him on the walk back to the truck. Once inside, he examined the dashboard and turned the ignition. The engine hummed on.

"Why are they here?" Slope said. "No way do those guys look inexperienced, and the storm won't come for a while. They want to stay in the cove, come hell or high water." He backed up and pulled the truck out with a jerk. "Something ain't right."

The sky looked low and fierce. If Slope had his way and the crew set sail, Vivienne would be out on the water, possibly battling a storm. Gray allowed his head to fall back on the neck rest.

"Let them stay," Gray said. "But insist they check into Drifter's Lodge instead of staying on board. The weather is unpredictable, and I disagree with you. As an experienced sailor, I can spot amateurs a mile away. Those two men can't handle rough weather."

"No skin off my back if they go missing."

"Think of all the paperwork."

Slope kept his eyes on the road. "I'd like to know who owns *The Isabelle*. Not those two, that's for sure."

The same thought had crossed Gray's mind. He didn't dare phone Vivienne. She would contact him when she could.

Within a day, his relaxed and boring vacation had transformed into something complicated and dangerous. It just went to show: be careful what you wish for.

Slope's phone burred within his jacket. "What?" he shouted, breaking the hands-free driving law he had given out so many tickets enforcing. "Are you fuckin' kidding me? No! I'll be right there."

He hit the accelerator, hard enough to slam Gray's seatbelt into his chest, turned on his wailing siren, and shouted:

"I'm not gettin' two minutes to rest today. Didn't even get to finish my breakfast. Your girlfriend has gone crazy."

"What? I don't have a girlfriend, Slope. Who are you talking about?"

"Dr. Emerald Kaur, who else? She's threatening to chop residents up with an axe."

Gray turned and took a last look at the yacht receding in the distance. With the truck now atop the winding cliff, he could just make out Vivienne moving on the deck. She grew smaller as he reluctantly moved further away.

Whatever she was up to, it would have to wait, but that concerned him.

Thirty feet from the boat, the cove's namesake blow hole bubbled and spurted its jet of streaming water up and out into the sky.

A similar torrent surged inside Gray. Something was about to go very wrong.

CHAPTER SEVEN

GRAY TOOK A FORTIFYING breath. Events at the body farm seemed to have spun out of control, and it was up to him to calm everyone down.

So much for keeping the scene of the alleged crime relatively uncontaminated.

They swung past the open gate in the SUV, and immediately a mob of women swarmed the vehicle, pointing back towards the farm, one of them yelling: "She has an axe! Crazy woman has an axe."

Whipping past the protesters, Gray ran, with Slope at his heels, passing the cabin, smelling the rot before the sites came into view, and stopping suddenly before Emmy's drenched and stiff figure, poised to strike.

She looked as surprised at the axe in her hands as the women around her. With a sinking stomach, Gray noticed the familiar face to the right. How had she gotten here so fast, and who was running the bistro?

Sita glared at him. Scavengers circled overhead.

Good thing this wasn't officially his case. But hiding behind civilian armor wasn't an option either.

"Put the axe down, Dr. Kaur," Slope yelled. He'd pulled out his gun and aimed it at Emmy.

"Slope," Gray said. "That isn't necessary." But the weapon remained fixed in the sergeant's hands.

Emmy didn't relent. "I'll put it down when these people get off my land."

"This isn't your land." Farrah edged closer to Emmy.

Slope ordered her to stay back.

Things were spinning out of control. Gray grabbed Farrah's arm. "You're leaving, now."

She yanked it back, giving him a disturbing smile he didn't wish to interpret. "I'm not."

"Unless you want someone to get shot today, you're leaving."

"Oh, I'd very gladly watch her get shot, Chief Inspector."

"Slope, tell the others to back off," Gray said.

But the sergeant kept his weapon aimed at Emmy, who stood in the middle of an ever-growing circle.

The situation threatened to explode at any second. And all for what? A bunch of rotting corpses and bruised egos. Or was Gray wrong about that?

Even Sita shook her head and refused to back down.

"Slope," Gray yelled.

"The second I lower this gun," the sergeant said, "she'll go nuts."

"No, she won't."

The circle was shrinking.

Emmy slashed the air with her axe. Several of the protesters, including Sita, screamed and moved back – except Farrah, who plunged forward.

Just as Emmy threw down the axe – just as Slope began to fire.

Gray jumped between Emmy and the shots, slamming her into the ground and narrowly dodging a bullet. She yelled out in pain, but didn't look hurt.

"Are you out of your goddamn mind, Slope?"

The Sergeant ran towards Emmy. "You're under arrest."

"No, she's not. They trespassed on her land, damaged her work."

Slope moved the handcuffs back to his belt and pinned down Emmy. "Don't do that again on my watch. You understand?"

Her slight nod would have to suffice. Watching Farrah's receding figure, she stood, shaking, her jaw and fists clenched.

Nothing at the body farm would now be admissible evidence. Farrah's minions had trampled over everything Gray and Seymour wanted preserved for SOCO. Anything they found might give them information, but the opposing counsel would argue that a stampede had charged through it, and they'd be right.

A more disturbing thought struck him. His eyes narrowed over the multitude of receding figures.

Was the timing of this protest a coincidence, or a deliberate attempt to sabotage evidence? He must find out who had incited this protest. Farrah Stone? That seemed too obvious. Any of the women, or some third party for that matter, could have egged her on. This group had a local reputation for acting before thinking things through, without trying to find common grounds or solutions.

Gray made certain Emmy was okay, and then, with a sinking stomach, moved to the parking lot. Other damage control awaited.

Catching up with Sita at her car, he said, "Why did you get involved in this? Farrah Stone is a malicious —"

"Farrah's my friend. The only one I had when Noelle and I came here."

She threw the sign into her Jetta's trunk. "That was quite a touching and heroic act I just witnessed. I see you'd risk your life for hers."

He touched her arm. All the warmth of their earlier meeting at the café had vanished. Looking down at his scarred, damaged hand, she raised one eyebrow.

"Why don't you get that fixed? Maybe it would be of some use then."

He could tell her that he'd never get it fixed. That it remained the only tangible connection to his son — a talisman of that precise time; that exact place. But Gray didn't bother.

Sita slammed the trunk closed. "Whose side are you on?"

Slope had escorted Farrah and the other women to their cars. He'd said nothing to Sita, almost conspicuously avoiding a confrontation which might make him look bad. Instead, he'd left that pleasure to Gray.

"I'm not on anyone's side," Gray said. "In a murder case — "

"But this isn't your case. You're not in charge, so for once, you can't hide behind that, can you?"

Her tone sounded different from when they'd been a family. She wouldn't have criticized his work then. But had she thought it?

He pulled the hot, wet collar away from his neck. Losing his temper meant weeks of trying to piece together the fragments of their relationship.

When you went to hell and back with someone, saw the worst of them and yourself, you might make the return journey alone. Not all trauma was binding. Some of it killed.

60

"I'm your wife. I live here, not her. I have a business and livelihood to protect and a daughter to feed. I'm not some single antisocial doctor who complains when all she has to worry about is deciding what to order for takeout."

"No one's taking sides."

She crossed her arms. "That's the problem. We're your family. Who is she to you? Does it occur to you what having a body farm here does to my business, to the economics of this town?"

The thought had never entered his mind. He saw a possible murder, he saw the imperative of protecting the town from the Stitcher, but not from any economic consequences.

"Last week, a family of tourists had something fall on them, Gray. What do you think it was?"

He shook his head. His heart sank. There was no winning this, he could tell.

"A finger. A vulture dropped the tip of a rotted, decomposed finger, and it fell right in front of the mom's face onto the baby's stroller. She started screaming. She made a fuss you wouldn't believe – ask Slope – threatening to sue. The story spread to Vancouver, as a human interest piece. What do you say to that?"

Seymour's car pulled into the lot. Where the hell had he been all this time?

Gray should respond. He should tell Sita he understood, and that he was on her side – provide reassurance that her business and livelihood remained safe.

Seymour honked the horn and gestured towards the cabin.

"I have to go," Gray said. It seemed a dismissive reply, and with a desire to end the conversation, he thought of what else to say. "This is a crime scene, and it has been contaminated."

Her nostrils flared; her eyes narrowed. He had dug a deeper hole for himself with an already estranged wife. But tempering caustic words proved difficult. Three years' worth of nights dealing with Craig's death alone, of counting the cracks on the aged ceiling, made any placating words lodge in his throat. And he mustn't be diverted from the crisis at hand. Gray had to catch the Stitcher before someone else died. Otherwise, what kind of detective was he?

They'd rarely argued in the old days. Mainly, Sita had accepted things. And that had cost her the world.

Across the lot, Seymour stood by the cabin, speaking to Emmy. The two of them went inside.

Sita's eyes moved from Gray to the cabin. She'd mistaken his gaze for one of jealousy, which bordered a level of absurdity he wouldn't lower himself to defend.

"Let's talk later after we've cooled off," he said. "I'll come by the bistro."

"What am I other than a means to your daughter? You took away my life; you know that?"

"We could have dealt with the pain together."

"No. I couldn't look at you without seeing Craig. It's those bloody emerald eyes that both your kids inherited. But after two years of looking into Noelle's—" She swallowed. "Has someone replaced me in your heart, or something else? Tell me."

How could he tell her he felt numb? It seemed the ultimate betrayal. How could he hurt her like that?"

"Not now, Sita. Please."

His tone could have been — should have been — warmer, he knew. Ego had always been his trouble — otherwise, wouldn't his son still be alive? Gray's flaws had pushed them this far off their chosen path. The same thought might be flashing through her mind. But he had work to do, and he couldn't talk about this anymore.

"Of course, not now. You have a case to solve; an addiction to appease."

She got behind the wheel and slammed the door. Her car puttered away, the tires spitting mud in his direction. Some clung to his scarred hand.

Across the lot, Slope had disbanded the protest and appeared satisfied with his work. He should be pleased, having cast Gray successfully in the part of the villain. Score one to you, Gray thought.

The sergeant approached him with one eyebrow raised.

"Are you going to charge Farrah Stone with trespassing?" Gray said.

"No. Why should I?"

"That's what she did. If the protestors had marched outside the gate, that would have been fine. But coming inside, interfering with Dr. Kaur's research —"

"Now, there's no evidence they did that."

"Look around, Slope. We're on research land. Her specimens have been irreversibly compromised. Emmy wouldn't have pulled out a weapon if the protesters weren't damaging months of painstaking research."

Even as he spoke, Gray recounted Sita's words. That he'd taken Emmy's side. If Farrah were charged, Sita would be too. What the hell was he doing?

Slope held up a hand. "Okay, okay. I get it. Dr. Kaur lives here, and if this happens again, someone will get hurt. Maybe even Sita."

Gray saw red. How manipulative was this sergeant? And how very confident in his ability to take on a Chief Inspector.

Seymour came up from behind. "I've settled Emmy down," he said, glaring at Slope. "She's understandably upset. First the mutilated body on her farm, and now this."

Gray faced Slope. "Has anyone reported a male, thirty to forty years old, with long blond hair, missing from either here or the adjacent towns?"

"Nope."

"Then let's assume he's from Vancouver or farther out." Gray thought out loud. "He must have arrived here somehow. By the coastal bus? Unlikely. What would he use to get around town? No one manages these roads and mountains without a car."

The wind picked up and blew Seymour's thinning hair across his brow. "The killer could have disposed of the vehicle nearby. Worth looking into."

Slope shrugged. "I'll take a drive around."

Seymour's answering frown indicated he didn't anticipate much of an effort.

The sergeant turned towards his truck, waving as he left. "I'll see you boys around."

CHAPTER EIGHT

HE RAISED THE rolling pin above his right arm and whacked the ball of dough on the kitchen counter, jostling the cabinets on their hinges.

Again and again, he hit it, nearing the end of the twenty minutes of beating required to tighten the pain brié, the "crushed" bread of Normandy, literally named 'beaten bread.' It was great therapy.

Outside Gray's cabin window, the Pacific thrashed and bubbled, gestating an impending storm scheduled to hit British Columbia's Sunshine Coast. Inside, his giggling toddler twisted at the table, her dark curls bouncing, and one chubby arm slamming the antique pine.

It had been an exhausting day. Father-daughter time was what he needed. Nothing would interfere with this, he promised himself. Nothing.

Leaving the dough to rise, Gray joined Noelle at the table. And through some sense of guilt or longing or self-flagellation, reached for his phone and played the familiar video.

Craig's wide eyes stared at him from the screen. "Is Mommy going?"

Gray's voice replied in the video, "You kidding? She doesn't even want us to go."

"But it's three whole days, Daddy. I don't want to go away... sailing, I mean. I'll miss her."

"You'll live."

A piece of spaghetti flew onto the phone, making Gray jerk back to the present. Tomato sauce blurred the screen.

Touching the stop button, he wiped the phone clean before tucking it into his pocket. A drowning need pulled him forward.

"Let's go to the beach, Noelle. Before it gets too dark."

The winter air slapped his face as he stepped into the impending dusk veiled by mist. The beach lay about thirty meters behind the cottage. Gray held Noelle's warm, mittened hand in his bare fingers as they strolled across the mulch and leaf-strewn grass, still wet from the afternoon's downpour.

Noelle squealed when the expanse of sea and sky came into view, with the snow-capped Rockies in the distance. To his right, an undulating pine-covered incline extended as far as the eye could see.

To the left, large rocks and coarse brown sand – scattered with the inevitable geese droppings – stretched for a kilometer before curving into a cove leading into downtown Halfmoon Bay.

He breathed in the salty freshness. The smell of home, and the most beautiful place he'd ever been.

Noelle began singing a song from her preschool: "Make a circle, make a circle–"

In perfect pitch, just like her mother. Hearing the tune brought back a decade-old memory. Before him, endless water drew the eye towards a cobalt horizon, hiding what lay beneath.

She sang, "–big and round, big and round."

He no longer felt the need to control the world or anything around him.

"Everybody hold hands. Everybody hold hands. Now sit down. Now sit down."

He lifted Noelle over his neck. The little boots touched his shoulders, but she'd stopped singing. The little girl gave him a Mona Lisa – and then the crunch of footsteps over rocks sounded from behind.

Gray steeled his expression and turned. Seymour's ironic voice broke the silence.

"Am I interrupting a family reunion? As your doctor, I can't recommend this."

Gray lifted Noelle off his shoulders. "You're a forensic pathologist – the last person I want as my doctor."

Seymour kept pace as they headed back. "We need to discuss the case."

"Not during my time with Noelle. After. I plan to drop her back at Sita's for the night, just in case."

The swinging of Noelle's arms matched her skipping. She jumped into the inevitable puddle and squealed in delight, soaking herself to the knees and looking mighty proud of the accomplishment. Gray smiled.

Drifting smoke filled the night air. Dad must have lit the fire in the stone grate inside the cottage. It would be warm and welcoming, and Gray could dry Noelle out.

They continued towards the cabin, finally reaching the side door. Gray stopped and lifted Noelle, holding her squirming, drippy figure at arm's length. He carried her up the steps and let her run inside. Her giggles filled the room with warmth. Gray's dad, Lew, lifted himself from an armchair and shuffled behind her.

They'd have the bread he'd baked and a roast for Christmas dinner. For the next few hours, he'd get to be Dad. Just Dad.

And he loved it.

Much later, the ornate clock sitting above the mantle stuck midnight.

How many idle moments had Gray spent in this stone and wood room, staring at the ancient timepiece handed down by his grandfather to his father, watching the hands move, listening to the mesmerizing tick-tock?

He and Seymour needed to chew over that last bit of evidence Emmy had provided the previous night – following Gray's unsuccessful chase after the killer. She'd remembered something about the body.

"Is Dr. Kaur sure? Couldn't she be wrong? It all happened so quickly."

"She's sure," Seymour replied, raising one hand. "Scout's honor."

"You were never a boy scout."

"No, but I give the movement my qualified approval whenever I can."

Neither man spoke, both assimilating what Emmy had said and what it meant.

A shifting log crackled and sparked in the stone hearth.

Seymour sat in Dad's worn leather recliner, picked up a pipe lying on the side table, but had the good sense to put it back down. Dad was practically psychic when it came to anyone messing with his things, even when he was resting in his room.

"Cheers," Gray said, lifting his tumbler of Scotch. The burn going down his throat was welcome, almost needed.

Seymour brought the single malt to his lips, his Adam's apple bobbing up and down, and pushed back the recliner.

The doctor stretched out his lanky form. "Whether the killer intended leaving that bit of evidence, I can't say. More likely, it's an artifact of the struggle."

"Don't jump to conclusions. Why didn't Emmy mention the mark right away?"

"She didn't realize it was important. Finding a body can be a shock. All the details registered and needed time to be processed."

Privately, Gray wondered how much any corpse could shock a body farm researcher.

"Too bad the corpse disappeared, and we can't confirm. What could have made that small, linear cut Emmy noticed on the victim's neck?"

Seymour twirled the crystal tumbler, seemingly mesmerized by flashes from the fire which reflected from the square-cut surface.

"Assuming the man was choked from behind – a big assumption since I have neither ligature nor body – a watch could have made that cut, or a ring, a bracelet? Or maybe a pink healing crystal, since this is the West Coast? My guess is, if the killer is right-handed, he'd wear, say, the ring on his left hand, and if he's left-handed, he'd still be wearing the ring on his left hand."

"What's more likely?" Gray asked.

"The latter. The dominant hand is more likely to be on top during the choke hold and therefore more likely to leave a cut. But nothing's carved in stone. We're making a ton of assumptions. I'd never swear to any of this in court."

"The ligature wasn't there."

Seymour's eyes narrowed. "Should it have been?" my dear James? Don't killers usually take the murder weapon with them?"

Seymour was playing Watson to his Holmes again. "Not all killers, Doctor. You know, Slope wears a diamond ring."

"Interesting."

Another log shifted and crackled, burning red and orange and blue. The rhythmic surf crashed outside the thick cedar walls – walls that kept the world at bay, for now.

Gray sunk further into the sofa, grateful for the warmth emanating from the hearth. He'd changed into dry sweatpants and a well-worn sweater and sat with feet inside wool-lined slippers.

How had he stayed away from his childhood home for this long? Away from this rustic, cedar-scented sanctuary: the humming, circling palms of the overhead fan; furniture oozing decades of ridged and marked memories; two kilometers of beach, flanked on one side by pine, birch, and tamarack between him and downtown Halfmoon Bay.

Gray downed the rest of the scotch in one gulp. "Why does the killer need to suture the lips?"

He hoped the mutilation came after the killing; the alternative was unthinkable.

"Serial killers sometimes leave trophies. They want to brag about the crime, want it recognized. They also crave media coverage so they can boast to themselves, alone if not in public. Fifteen years ago, did that killer suture the victim before or after death? Forensics would have known."

"After. I don't know if we're dealing with the same killer or if this is a copycat."

For a solid minute, neither of them spoke. Gray needed another drink. He rose and poured two fingers of single malt into each of their glasses.

Suddenly, the air felt hot and heavy. The main window overlooking the Pacific opened easily but with a creak. The rain may have ceased, but the rhythmic crashing of black, unseen waves thundered into the room, bringing with it the requisite saltiness.

Gray turned to face the room, enjoying the cool gusts of wind against his back. "The killer made an error in judgment. He or she didn't expect their chosen witness to be so observant."

Seymour leaned forward. "Chosen witness?"

"Someone left the body at the farm for Emmy to find. Then they removed it. Why? If the victim died at forensic site 144, why not move the body right away?"

"There wasn't time?"

"Or?"

"Or... the killer wanted the crime discovered, but didn't want the body examined too closely."

"Exactly."

Seymour shook his head and rose. He began pacing the room.

"There's another possibility. Emmy might have shown up before the killer had time to move the corpse. She discovers it and runs to call the police. The killer takes the victim away –"

"How do we know the crime was committed on site 144 in the first place? Think of her description, Doctor. The sprawled out hair, the legs at an obscene angle. The scene was staged. The murderer wanted the body found, but did they notice that cut? Timing is tight during a murder, and a killer runs on adrenaline. An inadvertent nick on the side of the neck might go unnoticed."

"Not by Emmy," Seymour threw in. "Choosing her as witness reeks of carelessness. The killer may see himself as invulnerable."

Gray indicated with his glass. "You and Dr. Kaur have a lot in common."

"How's that?"

"Neither of you can stand to see a patient alive."

"That hurts."

"You seem to like her."

Seymour blushed. "Actually, nothing has happened yet, but I hope—" He looked up at Gray. "Hey, you could stand to tone down the charm a bit."

"Have I been charming to Dr. Emerald Kaur?"

"No, you've been very Heathcliff. That's what worries me."

Lew James entered the room with his cane, and reclined in the chair Seymour hastily gave up. Lew's white hair was still tinged with the occasional blond, sticking upward, the relaxed and hanging lines on his face in contented repose as he lit and puffed an expensive cigar.

"Nice present, these are, son. Thanks. Have one; you too, Doctor." His glassy eyes narrowed. "You boys discussing the murder?"

"You heard about it, Dad?"

"I have my ear to the ground."

"But how? Slope doesn't believe there's been a death."

"Emmy phoned Teddy Atkinson since he owns the land, and Teddy called me."

Lew resumed puffing his cigar as though this explained everything before adding: "Of course, Teddy only confided in me because my boy's a famous detective."

Gray doubted that. As a renowned art expert, everyone held Lew James in high regard, including Teddy Atkinson, who probably wanted Lew's advice. Now that he lived here full-time, Dad was the calm, steady pulse of the small community of Halfmoon Bay.

"I need to speak with Teddy," Gray said.

"Naw, you don't. What makes you want to take the case on, Son?" Dad spoke casually, as though they were discussing the merits and shortcomings of a new local shop.

"Why would anyone leave a corpse at the body farm?" Gray said. "Only to remove it minutes later?"

"Sounds like a mystery. Guaranteed to cover up holiday boredom, I bet."

Tension entered the air; words unspoken but guessed. Did Dad disapprove of Gray's addiction to solving murders? Was he aware of the sutured lips?

"I know about the mutilation," Lew said. Silence hung in the air until he spoke again. "And what it means."

"Then you're two steps ahead of me."

"Not likely." Lew placed the cigar on the ashtray and straightened his chair. "Don't take on this case. It has nothing to do with you. You'd do better to go back to Vancouver early."

Seymour never could hold his tongue.

"James should stay and see the case through. Solve it with the most damage control. Otherwise, Slope gets unleashed like a bull in a china shop."

Rumor had it that the sergeant was more or less engaged to Teddy Atkinson's daughter. Maybe he had decided to save his future father-in-law from any hassles regarding the body farm.

Lew put out his cigar. He reached for his cane.

"You got other responsibilities now, Noelle for one. Things to figure out; healin' to do."

"And whoever sutured that poor man's lips together?" Gray said. "They just get away with it?"

"If it means a man taking care of his family, then yes. Kids come before chasin' criminals; when you gonna learn that?"

Dad gave him a look. Seymour pressed his lips together.

"You want me to leave my wife and daughter while a crazed killer roams Halfmoon Bay?"

Lew sighed. "I still think this is a bad idea," he said pushing up with the cane, just as the phone rang.

Gray answered it. The caller's scratchy voice spelled out its threat.

"Who is this?" Gray said, but the line went dead. He faced the two men. "Unknown number and too short a call to be traced."

Seymour stepped forward. "Well? What did they say?"

"The voice was disguised, but it sounded like a man – possibly over a cel phone. The reception went in and out."

Lew stood before his bedroom door, his shoulders stiff, his head held high. "And?"

"They threatened to hurt you, Dad." Gray slammed down the phone. "They threatened to hurt you unless I abandon the case."

Neither man spoke. A dog barked outside.

Gray closed the window and moved to the front door. "Stay here with Dad," he told Seymour.

He switched off the porch lights and stepped outside.

Nature hummed, expectant and waiting, concealing everything in a low-lying, grey mist. A gentle howl accompanied the steady surf. With the cloud cover, no one could see him, and he could see no one.

Keeping to the shadows meant staying close to the edges of the house. Ears attuned, Gray listened, but with all the collateral noise, he wasn't sure. Was someone running on the nearby asphalt?

He scanned the road. A faint shadow in the distance shifted before an engine roared. Headlights hit against dense fog.

Gray ran to his car and jumped behind the wheel.

Someone had called from a cel, as he'd suspected. Except they'd been standing before his house, looking at him through the window at the time. The killer had dared to come to his home.

The Lotus purred to life. Just as Dad stepped out the front door and called out for him to stop.

But Gray had already swung the car around, and now he sped up their road fifty meters behind the fleeing culprit.

He could barely keep sight of the vehicle with layers of mist obscuring the view. The steering wheel vibrated under his chilled hands. Blood pumped through his ears.

And he knew what lay ahead, and why Dad had tried to stop him.

The other vehicle took a right and climbed the inclining road. With so few cottages around, no rails had been placed between them and the rapidly lengthening drop down the edge of the cliff, to the beach below.

He was losing sight of the other car.

Gray stepped on the pedal. The wheels slid on the slick, wet surface. Two rights, then a left.

And now they were on a dirt road again, surrounded by darkness and trees. Foliage pushed inward from both sides, shrouding the sky above.

The fog was thicker here, and he couldn't see more than a couple of meters ahead. Not to his front. Not to his back.

Until he saw it.

And slammed the brakes and swerved. Sliding in a tortuous twist before the wheels gained traction, and he finally got control of the car.

Gray had come to a stop after a full hundred-and-eighty-degree turn. And he faced the deer who looked back at him, unblinking, before it leaped into the endless forest.

Sweat beaded his upper lip. The narrow road, sandwiched by fir, maple, and pine swam in a dense fog. He felt surrounded.

The case was now personal.

And entirely out of Gray's control.

CHAPTER NINE

THEODORE ATKINSON'S COVE-SIDE mansion resembled a pile of grey-brown cement blocks stacked together and decked with far too much tinsel. The ugliest houses required the most decorating to appear festive. Although once inside, Gray had to admit, the open central hall, the overhanging antique bronze and crystal chandelier, and the spacious formal salon on the right possessed rustic charm and even a certain proportional grace.

The stairs leading to the second floor were across the salon. "This way, my boy."

Teddy turned left into a long hall which curved at the end; he entered the first door on the left.

Stepping into the library after his esteemed host only reaffirmed Gray's impression of the house. Two long red sofas and several patterned wing chairs formed an elegant seating area. Under the bay windows straight ahead, a drinks trolley held every imaginable bottle of alcohol, and an antique rose wood desk beside it appeared suspiciously bare. The sea bubbled in the background.

The sense of home was palpable, but it was intermixed with an undercurrent of mystery afforded by the cove's checkered past.

Pine Cove had a dubious reputation a century ago, back in the time when the vibrantly papered walls and ornate furnishings added a gentle contrast to the roughness of the adjacent ocean and the lawlessness of the day.

"Too early for a drink, but I'm having Mrs. Benoit make us a kale and dandelion smoothie." Teddy's sixty-year-old jowls jiggled as he spoke, the loose flesh an unfortunate genetic trait sent down the generations — a fact confirmed by the nearby hanging portrait of Teddy's grandfather. "She refused to make 'em when I first brought her here from Paris. But this is the West Coast, I told her. We have our lawn clippings before our coffee in the morning."

Gray couldn't disagree. In Vancouver, you hiked "The Grind" or swam the cold English Bay after such a drink. But the evenings were different. After dark, people drank — sometimes a lot — though Gray never had more than one or two, and his penchant was for single malt scotch, not the usual beer.

The drinks arrived. Teddy handed Gray a tall glass. The jovial yet suspicious man also wore a class ring on the third finger of his right hand, one that came to a sharp point in the middle.

"Thanks, Mrs. B," he said, wetting his mustache. Green liquid stuck to the hairs before he wiped them away with a napkin.

It did taste of yogurt-drowned lawn clippings. Gray obediently gulped it down. During his family-man days, he'd make three glasses of some such concoction before anyone else awoke, and take his outside to the beach to drink with the rising dawn. He still did that, except now he did it alone.

"Your dad's a valued member of the community," Teddy said. "He's a leading art historian in BC. As his son, I offer you the same welcome in this house. In fact, why don't you come to our Christmas party, my boy? Your dad is invited, and bring that strange doctor fella of yours along."

"I'm here in a semi-official capacity. As you know, Emmy found a body on the forensic site, which subsequently disappeared."

"Yeah." Teddy put his glass down. "She called me, and I've gotten an earful from Farrah about that body farm, I can tell ya."

"Farrah Stone is against loaning out your land for forensic research. Many of the residents are. Do you regret doing it?"

"Nah. I do what I want, and no girl gets to tell me different."

The real Teddy was showing, beyond the formal host. Gray wouldn't precisely describe Farrah as a girl — not because of her age, but more because of her general demeanor.

Years ago, he'd accompanied Dad to her father's gallery and noticed her leaning against a wall in 5-inch red stilettos. She had reminded him of lemon and ice. Her ivory skin and platinum hair, not to mention her absolute stillness and focus, gave her an uncanny resemblance to the whitewashed stone statue positioned to her left. Two figures in stone.

He'd tripped over his untied shoes and maybe even drooled a little. Farrah's answering half-smile hurt more than if she had outwardly scorned his boyish interest.

"Do you believe Emmy?" Gray asked.

Teddy arched his back and stretched his broad form. His belly jostled in sync with his jowls and jutted out under the green plaid shirt. Gray decided he liked him. He admired any man who was his authentic self.

"Let's stretch our legs, Chief Inspector."

"Have you done much work to the house since the old days?"

"Sure. It's all updated–all except the cellar. That's my property manager Butch's terrain. We got a lot of old stuff that can't be thrown out."

They traversed the long hall, passing several closed rooms. It curved to the right and ended at a set of French doors leading to the back garden. Teddy must have twenty acres of land, all of which rimmed the Pacific on one side, including Pine Cove, and a small hill leading up towards Mount Eva on the other.

They wrestled the elements and walked along the open stretch of grass to a log cabin nestled at the far end.

"You're searching for suspects?" Teddy said.

"Anyone connected to the body farm. It wasn't a random place to dump a corpse. Plus, whoever made that body disappear was messing with Emmy's mind."

"You don't know that, Inspector. Seems like you're jumping to conclusions there. And without any evidence, a body even."

Gray kept in step with Teddy. "You're probably right. But I have to ask you–"

"What I was doing at that time? You want an alibi? Hell, sure. What time was it?"

"Without a corpse, we can't determine when the murder occurred. But the killer removed the body at 2 pm yesterday."

Teddy stopped mid-step. "Oh. I was nappin'." He met Gray's eyes. "Some people hike during the day; I nap. Need my beauty sleep, you know?"

They resumed their walk. Clumps of blueberry and raspberry bushes planted along the edges rustled in the wind, sweetening the air. It was a wonder Teddy didn't have brown bears as neighbors.

"Who would want to sabotage the body farm?" Gray asked. "Besides your fiancé and her entourage."

"Those women follow my Farrah around like she's some Messiah. You know, Dad served in the war, and he had a name for that kind of hard thinkin'–fascism, he called it. Couldn't say that out loud now without getting my head clubbed in. Those idiots think because they're hanging on the left side of the tree, they can't be fascists. Hah! Bunch of weaklings who can't think for themselves."

Gray breathed in and let it out slowly, grateful the other man didn't mention Sita. How would Teddy's marriage with Farrah pan out if that's what he thought of her? It seemed a bloodbath in the making.

"Where was Farrah yesterday afternoon?"

"Don't know. Let's ask her."

They'd reached the guest house. Several stone steps led down to the entrance. Teddy opened the wooden door unannounced. Inside, the sunken foyer was dimly lit, but the few steps up to the main cabin—currently used as a painting studio—revealed a bright space with vaulted ceilings and windows on all sides: windows to the sea, to the trees, to the mansion itself.

Teddy had barged in—the way he might enter a small child's playroom.

Farrah stiffened. She signed and held a paintbrush in mid air, poised as a weapon. Something told Gray this type of interruption happened often.

"How many times have I told you not to interrupt my painting?"

Several canvases leaned against one wall, all of them of the same scene: the immediate view overlooking the trees and ocean—all of them, somewhat amateur attempts to Gray's trained eye. Being an art expert's son had its advantages. If

Farrah had felt the artistic muse before their interruption, she had every right to be annoyed. That muse didn't visit often.

"Come on," Teddy said, his arms held wide open. "Gimme a kiss. You can return to your little paintin' later."

She turned an ever brightening shade of red, a world away from the ice princess yesterday at the body farm. Rage mingled with an odd vulnerability that was almost painful to watch. But Gray's work invariably intruded on this kind of privacy. He'd made his peace with that long ago.

Dad had once remarked on her father's firm hand in running the nearby gallery. 'Ice in his veins,' Dad had said. Jeremy Stone had a reputation for supporting only the best and most promising artists. Did he support his daughter's budding interest as a painter? Doubtful.

Teddy either didn't care or didn't notice Farrah's discomfort. Any artistic openness had shut down upon their arrival with an inaudible slam.

"I paint in the early mornings; you know that."

"Go back to it later." he waved a dismissive hand.

"That's not how it works. You're a businessman. You don't get it."

"And you're a businesswoman. When did you become an artist, eh?"

She noticed Gray for the first time since they'd entered. Her lips pressed into a thin line, one four-inch heel twisted and dug into the worn hardwood, and her every muscle looked tight and poised for action.

Teddy didn't seem to care. "Gray here wants your alibi for yesterday at two. When the killer paid Emmy a visit."

Farrah yanked her arm back and flung the dripping brush across the room. It hit the log wall and dripped hunter green tentacles down the wooden beams.

81

To Gray's right, Teddy sighed audibly. And added a careless shrug, as one might give a hard-to-break-in mare who refused to jump the requisite training hurdles.

This type of family dynamic only reinforced Gray's inclination to remain effectively single.

Farrah strutted over, her patent leather boots clicking on the pine planks. "I have the best alibi in the village, Chief Inspector." She lifted her chin and gave a wry smile. "One you're not even going to try and break."

"What you talkin' about?" Teddy asked. He seemed more impatient than Gray. "Who is it?"

"Sita James." She turned back to Gray. "Or, as she now goes by her maiden name, Sita Chand. We met at the spa and hot springs to go over our strategy for the protest." Farrah moved in closer. "She rubbed my back; I rubbed hers."

Gray didn't blink. "You take a lot of time off your day job."

"I pay employees at the gallery to hover around tourists who know nothing about art."

"That's no way to run a business, baby." Teddy moved towards her canvas. "Not bad. Could do better." He'd said the words lightheartedly, but they'd hit a sore spot.

Farrah said, "At least my family business came directly to me. Didn't skip a generation."

Teddy's neck stiffened; he turned beet red but was saved by approaching footsteps.

A new figure entered and stood poised at the doorway: his adopted daughter, Delilah Chen Atkinson.

She wore a black leather miniskirt and matching camisole and jacket. Every bit as beautiful as her soon to be step-mom, she also had the Atkinson attitude in full. An obvious affection existed between father and daughter, apparent in their exchanged look and raising of eyebrows at Farrah's expense. Farrah fumed.

"You're just getting in, I presume," Farrah said.

Delilah ignored the comment and slithered over to Gray, bringing with her a post-coital scent she hadn't bothered to wash away. It mixed with the paint fumes nastily. Teddy detected it too, and cleared his throat.

She cozied up closer and said, "Do you want my alibi, Chief Inspector Gray?"

"For all of yesterday afternoon."

Did Delilah think another man's scent would turn him on? Her naivety and clutching need to feel desirable saddened him.

He thought of Noelle le: the importance of having a father-figure in a young girl's life.

How had Teddy failed Delilah, and how could Gray avoid making the same mistake?

"I was with Reggie at his office," she said. "Ask him."

So, perhaps, the rumors he'd heard of Delilah and Sergeant Slope's unannounced engagement were true.

"Where were ya last night?" Teddy said.

She gave him a coy look. "Oh Daddy, I went out with friends. We just got back from Vancouver."

He didn't believe her, Gray could tell.

Delilah still had her eyes on Gray. "I love a dark and dangerous type."

"Delilah," her father warned.

"Don't worry, Daddy. This yummy Chief Inspector isn't on the menu. Right, Mummy-Dearest?" She'd turned towards Farrah who had proceeded to clean and pack up her brushes.

Gray had no intention of coming between the two. He focused, instead, on Farrah's earlier comment regarding Teddy's inheritance skipping a generation.

If Delilah had inherited everything from her adoptive grandfather, that fact went a long way toward explaining Teddy's accommodating attitude towards his daughter. Gray needed to discuss this with Lew. He'd know how the Atkinson fortune was dispersed.

"Where was Matisse at that time?" Gray asked Farrah.

"At the hot springs, of course. Matisse goes nearly everywhere with me; I'm his mother."

Wisely, neither father nor daughter commented.

On that note, Gray made his excuses and left. What a pitiful excuse for a family. Hell, who was he to judge? Delilah and Matisse were alive, weren't they?

He left the cabin and, outside, inhaled the tang of the sea, happy to get some fresh, unsullied air.

CHAPTER TEN

JOHN SEYMOUR FACED his friend and colleague across the wobbly, rustic table. "I might have made a decent criminal; a worthy Moriarty to your Holmes."

"Really?" Gray answered.

"You know what Conan Doyle said: When a doctor goes wrong, he's the first of criminals. He has nerve; he has knowledge—"

"He has tact."

"Do criminals need tact?"

"Often, yes."

"Then I'm out."

Gray scanned the dozen or so lunch occupants at My Alibi. "Vivienne called." He rested his chin in his left hand and rubbed his middle finger along the side of his nose. "She wants to meet."

"Took her long enough to get in touch with you."

Gray had apprised Seymour on what had passed earlier at Blow Hole Cove. It seemed this beach-side wilderness boasted cove after cove for hundreds of miles. How Seymour longed to return to his rented Vancouver condo overlooking the marina and city lights. Or better yet, to his small Victorian house back in Outremont, Montreal, where both he and Gray belonged. But for now, the excitement was here and so was Seymour.

"Where does she want to meet?" Seymour asked.

"At home, later tonight. The cabin's isolated enough that no one will see her."

Seymour stretched his legs under the retro-style table. The café's wooden seat hurt his butt and back.

He shifted. The seat creaked and groaned beneath him. "Tell your wife to get better chairs. Maybe a booth or two, for her more discerning clientele."

"For her older clientele, you mean. I tell Sita nothing." Gray held up both palms. "But feel free."

Seymour knew Sita well enough to reconcile himself to the uncomfortable chair.

His friend looked over the lunch menu and ordered a Provençale-style tartlet of snail fricassee with parsley garlic garnish. Seymour wrinkled his nose and opted for the Homemade smoked salmon, fresh vegetables, and truffle oil.

His coffee tasted dark and sour. "You know, coffee is acidic and dissolves dentin and enamel."

"I didn't need to know that."

"My knees are shot, my teeth are yellowing." Seymour examined his smile in the reflection of a stainless steel table knife. "I don't know how I'm going to make all these body parts last."

Gray's stylishly-cut dark hair matched his leather jacket, and with a little imagination he could pass for a high-priced hitman. Seymour could picture him in the role of villain as easily as inspector. Perhaps Gray had flipped a coin to decide between the two.

It must be exhausting being the redoubtable Gray James. He suddenly felt more relaxed, happy to be plain old John Seymour, affable if eccentric Forensic Pathologist. His patients were never demanding; his nonexistent wife never nagged; no brat sporting sticky fingers stained his clothes. All in all, life was pleasantly acceptable. And James seasoned it with just the right sprinkling of mystery and professional variety.

"Are we returning to the cabin?" Seymour asked.

"After we finish lunch and I ask Sita a question or two."

"So I'm a third wheel?"

"A fortuitous buffer."

"Hardly fortuitous. You brought me here."

Gray rubbed his temple. "Things became a little heated at the body farm."

"Was it about money?"

"No."

"Pecuniary matters aside, are you going to take her back? You know, that's what she wants. And I suspect there remains a certain subdued and magnetic attraction between you two."

Gray's emerald eyes bored into his. Noticing that his afternoon cappuccino – by Italian standards, a sacrilege after eleven am – was forming a cold film, Gray took a gulp. Apparently, no immediate response was forthcoming.

A customer opened the bistro door, bringing in a cold, damp draft which made Seymour shiver.

"She has a right to substantial child support," Seymour said, "given your net worth. I'm surprised it has taken her this long to corner you."

Seymour secretly resented Gray's aptitude for mathematics, and his success playing the cryptocurrency market. That three-million-dollar, water-view condo hadn't paid for itself.

"Sita knows I'll give her what she wants. She doesn't need to work or run this café. It isn't the money she's after."

"Then what?"

"A nuclear family. Getting accustomed to the other person's morning breath, and knowing how they spend each moment of their day."

"Sounds charming." Another solid tree of a man, chopped down to make a coffee table, a dresser, or this bloody uncomfortable chair.

It wasn't about independence, Seymour knew. He and Gray had something in common besides a morbid fascination with crime – they both clutched their privacy like a talisman. Both hated ever to have to explain themselves to others. Could Gray ever go back to that life?

Sita approached their table carrying two artistically arranged plates. His salmon with truffle oil smelled divine.

Once she'd seemed radiant to Seymour, with her ruby red lips, thick silk hair which brushed her waist, and petite, feminine figure.

Now, not the faintest of erotic notions fluttered across his mind, and he saw her analytically for what she was. A woman who blamed her husband – albeit not unfairly (from a certain point of view) – and a woman who would use her second child to now get that estranged husband back.

It didn't have the makings of a healthy family, but what did Seymour know? The last woman he'd dated dumped him because he couldn't salsa.

"I have an important question for you," Gray said. "About the case."

She set down the plates and clucked her tongue.

"Of course, you do. And here I thought you'd come to see me. We went through this at the Spook's farm –"

"That's unfair," Seymour said. "Why do people on the west coast act like they're still in high school?"

Sita met his eyes and glared. If looks could kill.

Behind her, Gray swiped a hand across his neck, indicating Seymour should shut up.

Well, he wouldn't. How dare this community college dropout mock a woman who graduated at the top of her medical school class? West coasters did indeed exist in continuous high school mode. Probably a result of all the readily available drugs.

Gray cut a piece of the buttery tart and dipped it into the garnish. "Ignore him," he said to Sita. "Firstly, were Farrah and Matisse with you all of yesterday morning?"

"Yes. We did a yoga class and a meditation session. Farrah needed it after everything Teddy's daughter is putting her through. And Matisse follows her everywhere like a goat on a leash. We relaxed afterwards at the hot springs."

Gray put down his cutlery and, in a characteristic gesture, rubbed his index finger against the side of his nose. "You're in the best possible position to tell me about any strangers visiting Halfmoon."

"We're a tourist town."

"Not this time of year. You'd notice a stranger with long blond hair. Maybe he wore it in a ponytail; I don't know. Anyone spring to mind?"

She pulled up a chair and sat, uninvited. Her leg even brushed against Seymour's. He resisted the urge to edge back.

"I remember a guy like that," she said. "A couple of days ago. A real pain in the ass. He wanted his salad dressing, croutons, and onions on the side. What's left? A head of lettuce?"

Gray perked up; his words came fast. "Did he mention his reason for visiting Halfmoon Bay?"

She scrunched her nose. "No. He complained about the food and left without leaving much of a tip."

"But he was here," Gray said, looking pretty pleased with himself, if a little slow.

Seymour jumped in. "Did he pay by credit card?" Honestly, who was the detective here?

"He paid cash. I remember the lousy one-dollar tip. "

"Any impressions?" Gray asked. "Local artist, snowboarder, here from Vancouver?"

"No, not an artist. If anything, he looked like that sharp but useless type who critiques other people's art and always finds it wanting."

Sita rose and hesitated, as though she might lean over and kiss Gray, but instead, she waved farewell and moved away.

Had Seymour seen frank hunger in her eyes? Hunger and regret? It didn't appear reciprocated.

Gray didn't seem to notice. Now that they'd confirmed the existence of a stranger who might be Emmy's body farm victim, action would follow.

Gray's phone burred, surprisingly playing no particular song. He had a customized ring-tone for everyone, but not yet for Slope, it seemed.

Seymour privately liked the ringtone Gray used for him: the theme song to his favorite Paul Newman movie, The Sting.

Gray listened to whatever the sergeant was saying, then answered:

"Who is the vehicle registered to? Donovan Price? No, I've never heard of him. Sita confirms that a stranger meeting the description ate here a couple of days ago. Which meant he stayed in town overnight. Worth checking the local lodge and nearby hotels to see if he met up with anyone."

Slope spoke on the other end for a long time, uninterrupted. The suspense bubbled inside Seymour. He put down his fork and knife with a clang.

"Where did they find the car? Tell me."

Gray held up his hand. "Dr. Seymour's with me now. Yes, I'll bring him" After downing his coffee, he worked quickly on the tart.

"They found a car within walking distance of town," Gray said, looking exceptionally pleased with himself.

The game was surely afoot.

CHAPTER ELEVEN

EMMY COULDN'T BELIEVE what she'd discovered about this pretty, peaceful little village. Who knew what lurked behind their mineral hot springs, their yoga retreats, their mid-winter music festivals.

She held her breath and opened her eyes, blinking to the sting of salt water.

The frigid current skimmed across her shoulders and bare midriff – the two-piece red racing suit wholly inappropriate to the water temperature; a wetsuit would have been better.

After the showdown with those local women at the body farm, only one thing could take away the internal churning restlessness; only one thing could calm her before she undertook what had to be done.

The waves soared above her and crashed downward, and provided a temporary reprieve from the fear that was her habitual companion.

No one currently walked the beach. Emmy now treaded water near the shore, where her feet could just touch the bottom, and recalled something Seymour had mentioned.

Somewhere off this shore, Gray James and his son had gone sailing. This was where it had happened.

Seymour had shared another fact (which made her wonder just how discreet he was) – he'd once caught Gray examining his open hands and rubbing them as though trying to remove a stain.

The clouds overhead seemed low enough to touch, their morphing gray surface sinister. She scanned the purple horizon, the bubbling sea, and the windswept brown sand.

Nature looked its best in this angry state -- like a wild, uncontrolled force that could wipe out all superfluous existence in an instant.

She fought the tide and dragged herself out of the violent surf. Her feet whipped pebbles and coarse sand behind her as she ran, arms tightly wrapped across her chest. She ran all the way back to her truck.

Inside, the damp had steamed the windows. Emmy's swimsuit stuck to her skin, and the dry clothes she pulled on felt rough and scratchy.

A few minutes later, she was looking past the fogged windshield and wipers sweeping from side to side. A parking space lay vacant, directly in front of her destination.

Farrah's art gallery looked open yet empty.

Inside, Emma was a child – which made facing recalcitrant adults particularly distasteful.

Her wet hair, that constant BC dampness that penetrated the bones, and the harsh weather made the twenty-foot sprint particularly unpleasant. The art gallery door swung open in the wind, and wet, colorful autumn leaves – magenta, yellow, and a few of them still green – swept in. The layer of debris littered the white marble floor.

Three white walls stood dotted with vibrant canvases: scenes painted by local aboriginal artists depicting summer, fall, winter, and spring around the coast and surrounding mountains. Modern sculptures stood strategically in the middle of the rectangular space.

Her nemesis leaned against a headless torso carved of local stone.

"What do you want?" Farrah said. Her bony face had such sharp edges; it was a wonder the skin atop didn't slice through. All the color in those cheeks came from carefully applied rouge. She wore a tailored white designer suit and a matching diamond set which could fund the body farm for a year.

"An explanation."

"You're not getting one. Now, get out before I call the police."

So the tables had turned.

"Your mindless entourage trampled two of my residents. They broke a limb I've been studying for months, and severed a skull from the neck. And worse, I must disclose the incident in my results, and explain it to my colleagues at the university."

"Yuck," Farrah said, snarling. "How can you talk about rotting corpses like that? You and your colleagues should be ashamed doing such awful research. Have you no respect for the dead?"

"Good people donated their bodies to science. They trusted the institute, trusted me."

"And you failed them," Farrah shouted. Her lips reassumed their wonted thin frigidity.

"I didn't. You're guilty of assault. Months of research got contaminated. Do you have any idea what you've done? Those two bodies represented an integral part of the project. The loss can't be corrected."

"Good. Then you'll close done and crawl back under your rock."

The reality of the situation was becoming increasingly clear to Emmy. Slope wouldn't defend her or the farm against this woman – not while he had his eye on Delilah Atkinson. She must take care of this herself.

A flush ran up her face. Rage lodged within her throat, making it hard to breathe. We all had a monster within us – one that was capable of murder.

The gallery lay quiet enough to hear a pin drop. Two employees watched them from the sidelines, unmoving.

Emmy spoke softly. "If you cause any more damage to my facility, I'll burn this gallery down."

"Did you just threaten me?"

"Yes."

Was it time to mention the other fact she'd uncovered? What Seymour and the Inspector must surely know.

No wonder the Inspector had flipped out when she'd described the body lying dead at the facility. The entire town would dread such horrid evil returning to their supposedly idyllic community.

"Teddy told me," Emmy said through clenched teeth.

Farrah widened her stance. The bony legs looked fragile enough to snap. "What did my fiancé tell you?"

"About the body found fifteen years ago, not far from my premises."

"Just spit it out."

"Don't you know about it? Didn't he confide in you? Tell you about the unsolved murder fifteen years ago?"

"I don't have to listen to this. Get out."

"Careful," Emmy said, taking a step forward. The other woman's strong and fruity perfume bugged her. She hated perfume. "Or you might become the next victim."

Farrah looked stunned. Might as well bring the threat home.

"Or you might have your lips expertly sutured together with 4.0 surgical nylon."

CHAPTER TWELVE

THE THINGS WE LEAVE behind after death don't represent us, Gray thought.

While stooping under a tarp tied to trees on all four ends, he delved into the overnight bag found in the trunk of the abandoned Honda Prelude.

Slope's men had found the car a mere kilometer from town, hidden away on the outside edge of Beaver Road which traced the outside of a small man-made lake.

In the sixties, a mountain stream had been dammed up to form Beaver Lake – to provide a tranquil water setting for the two dozen surrounding cottages. Species of trout, bass, and kokanee had been introduced, along with the appropriate vegetation. A thriving ecosystem had formed and flourished. Gray knew the lake well.

Rain pounded the tarp; wind ruffled the sides, whipping the plastic corners and rippling the surface in crisp rhythmic beats.

Gray heavy and rushed lunch sat like a brick in his stomach. Despite donning his waterproof winter coat, he felt the cold and dampness prickle his skin.

"Not much here," Slope said.

Gray unzipped the black leather bag. Inside, a toothbrush, toothpaste, a hair brush, and various other toiletries filled a side compartment. A crisply pressed chambray shirt and a pair of relaxed fit jeans lay in the bottom. Nothing else. Only enough for a night away, two at most. Gray found no phone, no laptop.

They were too close to town. The presumed dead man, Donovan Price, might have visited any of hundreds of nearby houses before his death. Nothing in the car helped to narrow down the search or explain why he'd come to Halfmoon Bay, and who he might have seen.

Gray almost wished they'd found the vehicle further up the mountain. That would have narrowed the possibilities of where Price might have encountered his killer.

As it was, Price could have met anyone, anywhere near town. Hell, the killer might have moved the car afterward. So where did that leave them?

"Emmy wasn't lying," Gray told Slope.

The sergeant had the nerve to look entirely unapologetic — annoyed even — almost as though Gray, Emmy, and Seymour had personally delivered this evil to his serene village.

"Yeah, Price might be dead," Slope said, waving a careless hand. "But who'd kill him and then remove the body from that god-awful farm?"

"These are questions you should have asked before rain and residents ruined the crime scene," Seymour said. He'd silently crept up from behind. "This lake smells. And frogs keep jumping up at me."

Gray put down the bag. "Find anything in the vicinity, Doctor?"

"On preliminary examination, nothing to indicate a murder happened nearby. But SOCO will find something in this jungle. They always do. Even if it's a discarded condom from the summer."

Gray gave him a look. Seymour shrugged.

"I want that email from the first missing girl," Gray said to Slope.

"What?" the sergeant said.

"The first alleged victim — the babysitter found by a child — you told me about her in the café."

"Oh yeah," Slope replied. "I'll get on that. You're taking an awful lot of interest in this case."

"Whatever keeps me away from cabin fever, Sergeant. You'll get there one day yourself."

"Oh, I'll never become a workaholic. I don't have that flaw."

He dared to look smug.

After Slope left, Seymour nearly jumped out of his skin with excitement. "I'm coming with you."

"No."

"You have a name now. And an address from the car registration. Instinct tells me we're driving to Vancouver today."

When Gray moved to protest, Seymour held up a hand. "You know I'm right."

"The sea to sky drive won't be pretty, John. Hell, it's out and out dangerous in this weather. And there's the ferry ride in between."

"We're both Vancouverites now. Sort of. What's a little spitting rain?"

Seymour had purposely misunderstood him. "Not on the way there," Gray said. "I'm referring to the way back. Things could suddenly worsen even if the storm isn't due for a couple of days. I'm coming back come hell or high water to meet Vivienne at the cottage. Are you sure you want in?"

"Absolutely," Seymour said, straightening.

They took the Sunshine Coast Highway 101 South to Horseshoe Bay.

He'd taken Dad's truck instead of the Lotus, much to Seymour's relief, who looked a little green, glancing at the near vertical drop from the passenger side of the car. It led straight into the ocean below. Surf and sky stretched out as far as the eye could see, and faded into a cobalt horizon.

The winding highway always intimidated those unaccustomed to its twists and turns, but Gray had spent his teenage summers here. He'd traveled this road countless. What was a little rain?

"Take it slow," Seymour said. "No one's racing you there, James. The man's dead. We have plenty of time to sift through his underwear drawer."

"On the other hand, we're not getting any younger."

"Speaking of age, how old is your dad? He shouldn't be smoking cigars."

The last thing Gray needed was a lecture on medical risk factors and life expectancies.

Seymour perked up. "Lew reminds of a joke I once read: What did grandpa say before he kicked the bucket?"

"I'm afraid to ask."

"How far do you think I can kick this bucket?"

Gray counted to ten.

"I don't have permission for a search," he said. "The Vancouver office can't know."

"You could get a warrant."

"In a couple of days. By then, we get rained out at Halfmoon Bay, and the Stitcher strikes again."

The Horseshoe Bay-Langdale ferry was still running. Rain spat on the windshield, and the wind howled around them as the ferry circled around Bowen's Island to dock in West Vancouver. Traffic was light through Stanley Park and they drove alongside the seawall down Beach Avenue.

"That's your condo, right?" Seymour said, pointing towards a high balcony overlooking Granville Island and English Bay.

"I've owned it for years," Gray said. "It was an investment."

They crossed the bridge to the other side of the bay and reached Donovan Price's Kitsilano basement apartment. The surf and Kitsilano Beach were just visible through the narrowly stacked houses. Even in a bay, the Pacific thrashed.

The doorbell sounded harsh in the quiet of the darkened street. No answer.

The lack of house keys presented no obstacle. Gray jimmied the lock within fifteen seconds.

"This area is damn expensive, even to rent," Seymour said, both of them aware that the average Vancouver bungalow by the beach went for four million dollars.

The one-bedroom, low-ceilinged apartment hadn't been renovated since the eighties. Gray recognized the style of the tiled kitchen countertop, the parquet floors, and yellow backsplash from his childhood. He secretly liked the retro look but wouldn't admit that in front of Seymour.

Despite the dated decor, the space possessed an air of forced order, to the point of obsession. Every piece had its place, and no knick-knacks or mementos littered the tables or shelves. The apartment could have been a corporate rental, containing nothing besides the necessary dishware and clothing needed for a brief stay.

"Let's look for any clues about his profession," Gray said. "Better to know tonight than wait to hear back from the department."

They'd put in a call to Vancouver headquarters to get all information available on Donovan Price, which wasn't much since the victim had no form or even a parking ticket to his name, let alone a police record.

A squeaky clean citizen if Gray had ever seen one. So how did that kind of man get himself violently killed?

Price's bedroom was as bare as a monk's. The bedside drawers contained nothing of interest, except for one single photo tucked amongst a pile of pressed shirts.

Gray picked up the black and white snapshot, its edges graying and crumpled from generations of handling.

The picture was of an abstract painting; one Gray failed to recognize. Still, the style of the work seemed familiar, but he couldn't put his finger on it. Dad probably could.

Without giving it a second thought, he slipped the photo into his jacket pocket.

Seymour entered the room and raised his eyebrows. Gray showed him the snapshot, but he didn't recognize the abstract either.

"Anything else?" Gray asked.

"Nothing. It's as though the man doesn't exist. More likely, he had OCD. There's nothing superfluous left to collect dust. You know what I mean? All documents online, all personal photos scanned, none printed or hanging etcetera. I would have expected to find more of the pink underwear, at least. Even his fridge has a single used carton of milk.

"Has it expired?"

"Not yet."

"He wasn't in Halfmoon Bay for long, then." Gray stroked his jaw. His stubble felt itchy. "Let's find Price's computer, if he has one."

"It's not here, James. And no one would leave a computer in their car during the winter."

"Meaning we might never find it. The killer took care of the phone. There's no desktop here, so he wasn't a gamer."

Seymour tried one last tack. "What if Price had an office elsewhere?"

They spoke to a few of the neighbors and garnered only one fact: the victim had a sister. Otherwise, no one knew a thing about him.

"Let's go to headquarters. I want to look him up myself."

Seymour said nothing. He sat silently in the car on the drive to the VPD office on Cambie Street.

Once at his desk, Gray performed an online search. "Price is a freelance art critic," he said. "He writes for various starving hipster publications, meaning he couldn't afford a parking spot in Kitsilano, let alone a basement condo."

"People inherit money. Any relatives?"

"No way of knowing. I'm looking at one of his articles on the decline of modern art. Pretentious fluff."

"We shouldn't speak ill of the dead," Seymour chided.

One of the articles showed Price posing with his sister.

"Hah," Gray said. "Talk about opposites. Sarah Price not only has a police record we know her well."

"I recognize the name."

The doctor would remember soon enough. Meanwhile, with Sarah's number and address copied for future reference, Gray thought about what to procure from his West End condo before returning to Halfmoon Bay.

"I remember," Seymour said, slamming the table. "That scandal with the last police commissioner and a certain high-priced prostitute. That's her?"

"Yes. Price isn't a common name, but it isn't rare either. I didn't make the connection until she came up."

A lengthy phone call with Sarah yielded little. Donovan loved the city and despised nature. She hadn't seen her brother in over a year and didn't know why he'd ever visit Halfmoon Bay.

A half hour later, Gray pulled the truck up in front of his condo building.

Twenty years ago, these small apartments overlooking the Pacific were prestigious rentals, until skyrocketing Vancouver prices had sparked their conversion into high-end condominiums.

From his twelfth-floor apartment, Gray had an unimpeded view of English Bay. A wall of ceiling to floor windows ran across the living room and master bedroom.

He never grew tired of the view; never saw it as routine or ordinary. And now, when fifty-kilometer winds blew the salt water into white-tipped peaks which crashed onto the coarse sandy beach, it looked more magnificent than ever.

Gray opened the sliding glass door and stepped out onto the balcony. This high up, the wind blew harder, and Vancouver was lit like a Christmas tree, with artsy Granville Island on the left, and Kitsilano immediately across.

But it was the wild Pacific that drew the eye to a violet horizon—that seemed to have all the answers; that seemed to belittle all problems.

He inhaled the salty air. Anything might happen on a night such as this. Anything.

Seymour stepped back. "I don't like the way all these glass walls are shaking. You sure it's safe? That glass could snap under all this wind pressure and slice right through us."

"We all have to go sometime. You haven't visited my place during a storm, have you?"

"No, and I don't like it."

How often had Gray sat in this very spot, riveted by the uncontrolled frenzy of nature, the shaking of the floor to ceiling panes which could shatter at any moment?

That he should enjoy such weather made no sense.

"Look at these." Seymour stood drooling before a wall of original classic movie posters. "*His Girl Friday, The Big Sleep, North By Northwest.*" He removed his glasses and leaned in to examine each image up close. "These are fantastic. I knew we had more in common than dead bodies."

"Let's not waste time. I'll be back in a second."

Gray entered the larger of the two bedrooms, which was only ten by eight feet. The safe in the closet contained the item in question. He retrieved the metal object and tucked it into his pants pocket. Seymour stood at the threshold.

"You know, Cary Grant was Hitchcock's favorite comedic actor. Fortunately, the director's blonde fixation didn't extend to the male lead – or Paul Newman might have found himself crawling on Parisian rooftops in *To Catch a Thief.* I believe Tippi Hedrin, by the way. Genius or not, Hitchcock seemed a dark man to me."

"Doctor–"

"You sounded just like Cary Grant when you said that."

Gray counted to five.

Seymour's voice lowered. He pointed towards Gray's pocket. "Don't bring that, James."

"It's a police revolver. I'm a policeman."

"Not really. You're as much a suspect as any of the residents at Halfmoon Bay."

Gray tried to pass, but the doctor stopped him. "Gray by name, gray by nature?"

"Must be."

During that last case in Montreal, when everything was against Gray – even then, he'd refused to compromise his beliefs and resort to using his gun. And now, that resolve had broken, but why?

The answer was clear. Gray had no intention of losing anyone he cared about to a crazed killer. Not now. Not ever.

He shook himself free.

"Small bedroom, isn't it?" Seymour said. "Still, I bet it gets the job done." He might as well have winked.

"Maybe you should request to be officially assigned to the case," Seymour said.

"Not during the holidays. It would ruffle Slope, and whatever cooperation I've gained from him would disappear. Maybe after Christmas. If the Stitcher's still at large."

"Oh, he will be," Seymour said. "I'm psychic that way."

Gray strode out of the bedroom, but Seymour wasn't stopping.

"I know you can shoot a man between the eyes from a hundred yards away. I've seen your file. You'd be tried as a professional if you discharged that weapon."

Gray laughed. "In the way a trained boxer would after a bar brawl?"

"Yes. You can't use a gun off duty."

Gray got his coat and waited by the door.

He got into the driver's seat. Seymour hadn't spoken on the way down the elevator, but the narrow space inside the vehicle was thick with tension.

Once they were back on the winding highway, with the turbulent water to their left, Seymour finally said:

"You're not going to delve into the Stitcher murder fifteen years ago, are you?"

Gray kept his cards close to his chest. "I don't think it's relevant."

"What about the other recent victim, the babysitter whose body disappeared?"

Time was tight. Gray could feel it in his bones. "Slope didn't forward the email the missing girl had allegedly sent to her family. Getting the full story from the family is imperative. I'll speak to them myself.'

"Let me. You have Slope, Vivienne, and that whipper-snapper of a wife to handle. You slice a Chief Inspector into too many pieces, and nothing gets done."

"We don't know if the babysitter is dead or not. If Slope's right, she's traveling abroad and doing fine. If he's wrong, then how do we find the body?"

Gray glanced at Seymour's profile before returning his gaze to the treacherous road.

The headlights shot oblong beams over the paved, winding highway, catching the wall of rugged rock to the right, and the near-vertical, hundred-foot drop into the ocean to the left.

Lights from oceanfront apartments and beach houses twinkled in the distance across the black bay, like candles flickering. They passed all this— until they were well out of town, and only the winding highway and dark, endless ocean stretched out before them.

Out here, the full force of the wind shook the truck, hard enough that the wheels lost their grip once or twice, making Seymour clutch the edges of the seat.

There wasn't much rain, but the wind could dislodge large chunks of rock and send them hurdling onto the truck. That sort of thing happened every year. You accepted it as a Vancouverite, the way you accepted earthquakes, taxes, and universal healthcare.

Gray shifted, adjusting his cramped back while salt-tinged air blasted from the vent onto his face. The treacherous drive wasn't the only thing bothering him.

Usually, he felt comfortable around Seymour, but something about the doctor's manner made the inside of Gray's mouth prickle. He swallowed.

"You're hinting at something," Gray said. "I don't know what it is."

"Sure you do."

For the moment, neither man spoke.

Gray broke the silence. "I'm not a bad man."

"No, I'd say you're an exceptionally good man."

From time to time, each of them goaded the other — neither expecting the other to be a good man, only an interesting one.

"Life exists in shades of grey. There are people I have to protect."

"And you've been singled out by the killer in more than one way."

Gray's throat went dry. The tips of his fingers itched.

He felt Seymour's eyes upon him, turned and saw the intensity in the glittering irises.

"We don't need to discuss it, James. I'll visit the first victim's family tomorrow if you like. And get the email she allegedly sent to Slope."

Seymour rested his head back to take a nap, leaving Gray to spend the rest of the drive in pregnant silence.

CHAPTER THIRTEEN

BY THE TIME Seymour and Gray made it back to the cottage, the doctor had taken on a peculiar shade of green. He gripped the rail while taking the wooden steps of the cabin one at a time, and brought a hand to his mouth.

No boulders had broken off the ascending cliff lining the highway during the drive, and they hadn't slid off the road and over the cliff side into the bubbling stormy sea.

Now, they were home. Safe and sound. And soon, Seymour would have his salmon-like coloring back.

Gray unlocked the wooden door with his old key. First, the warmth and light from the fire hit him, followed by a woman running into his arms.

Vivienne — who invariably evoked within him an impression of chocolate and spice.

He needed the hug as much as she did. But she trembled in his arms. Was she holding back tears? Vivienne never cried.

"I couldn't believe it when I saw you on that yacht," Gray said, gripping her bony shoulders. She'd lost weight. "Why were you with those two men? You should be back in Montreal."

She pulled away from him and smiled. "Chief Inspector," she said, always addressing him formally when on a case, despite their longstanding friendship. So, she was on a case after all. "It's so great to see you."

Vivienne turned to acknowledge Seymour, who had slumped into Dad's chair. He invariably monopolized it when Lew James wasn't around, and then jumped up innocently when the rightful occupant returned.

How had Vivienne gotten inside? Lew must have let her in and gone out.

"Nice to see you, doctor," Vivienne said in that perfect English, tinged with musical Québecois intonations that made Gray feel homesick for Montreal.

She turned back to Gray. "I need a drink before the interrogation. Is it too early in the evening?"

"Never too early for my favorite detective."

"I thought I was your favorite detective," Seymour said, looking and acting more like himself.

Gray moved to the drinks cabinet. "You're my favorite butcher."

"Ouch. I have never used a cleaver in my life. My incisions, I'll have you know, are both accurate and precise."

Gray poured himself and Seymour the usual scotch. Vivienne, he knew, drank only wine. Grabbing Dad's open bottle of Chianti from the fridge, he retrieved the largest wine glass in the cottage and filled it to the rim.

"Whoa," Vivienne said. "Are you trying to get me drunk?"

"Drunk enough so you won't return to the yacht, I'm guessing," Seymour supplied, hazarding a look at his friend.

"Let's all sit down," Gray said. "I need some answers, even though I have no right to ask you. Both Seymour and I are your friends. And we're worried."

Dad must have brought out some croissants for Vivienne before he went out. A plate of them sat on the coffee table, and a few betraying crumbs indicated she'd had one.

"Doctor?" Gray said, holding out the tray.

"Not me." Seymour patted his slightly flabby midriff. "I'm watching my figure."

Gray picked one up and took a buttery bite. The requisite flakes fell onto his lap; Sita used the most authentic French recipes, striking the perfect balance between salt and sweet.

Vivienne gulped the wine faster than he'd expected. He didn't dare mention her soon-to-be ex-husband — or the incredible turn of events which had marked both the end of their last case in Montreal and her marriage.

Once, the four of them had been friends: Gray, Sita, Vivienne, and Saleem. Now, both marriages had disintegrated to something unrecognizable.

"Have you seen Sita?" he asked.

"She's changed." Her irises twinkled in the firelight. Her restless shifting caused the old sofa to creak. Vivienne measured her words always, especially around him — not wanting to hurt, not wanting to rub a raw spot.

The two women were once inseparable, before the accident. For years, Vivienne blamed him for Sita's disappearance; she'd lost her a best friend, and now, her husband — in part because Gray had solved that last case, and produced that shocking link.

All she had left was Gray — perhaps not much of a conciliation prize for what she'd lost. Vivienne must feel as abandoned as he had by Sita. Would she forgive more easily?

Vivienne cradled her large glass, sitting on the sofa chair opposite Seymour. Her hands appeared steady; her face serene. The fire lit her delicate features and the tips of her short brown hair.

She looked pensive.

"What it is?" Gray said.

"She's not the same."

"What do you mean?"

Even as the words left his mouth, he knew he didn't need to ask. Didn't he feel the same thing?

"I've only met Sita a couple of times since I've been here," Vivienne said. "Diego keeps a pretty good watch over everything I do. I kept looking for that woman who was more than a sister to me, and she's not there. The eyes are empty."

Gray took a seat across from her. "She did what she had to do to survive. It isn't her fault, it's mine."

Vivienne didn't correct him. Sugar coating wasn't her way. But there was no blame either, and that seemed new. Only acceptance – maybe because she'd finally forgiven him, or because he was all she had left of the old days.

"Noelle," Vivienne said. "She is all you, mon cheri."

"But how are you, really?" Gray asked.

She smiled. "I'm surprisingly good. Getting away from Saleem and all that drama was the best thing for me. I can live my life on my terms now. It gave me the stamina to accept this undercover operation. After this, a promotion isn't farfetched. Maybe even the RCMP, although they aren't in Quebec."

So it was the opposite of what he'd thought. She wasn't suffering; she was healing – and finding her new life. Gray could not have felt happier for her. But he also wanted her to stay safe. He thought of that historic stereotype of the Royal Canadian Mounted Police on horseback. Vivienne was allergic to horses – and the outdated stereotype no longer applied to most officers. Instead, being with the RCMP meant you had jurisdiction over most of Canada, not just specific provinces.

Seymour jumped up. "Yes, yes, but what about the yacht, Vivienne? Tell us about that."

"The look on your face at the cove," she said to Gray, taking a gulp of wine and smiling.

"Glad you find me amusing. What's it all about?"

She took her time, obviously enjoying dragging it out – as the doctor often did – at Gray's expense. He put his feet on the coffee table. Might as well enjoy the single malt.

Never chase a woman, Dad had taught him. Never chase a witness, he'd learned from his work. Let both come to you. He applied this to Vivienne now, if only to stop himself from leaping over the table and shaking her.

"Art," Vivienne said.

Gray straightened. "What?"

"Art. You have a smuggler in this town of yours, Chief Inspector. And I have the unpalatable job of finding him, or her."

"The smuggler lives here, in Halfmoon Bay?" Seymour asked. His tone suggested that any successful criminal should choose a more cosmopolitan residence.

"Absolutely. And it's someone with power."

Seymour slammed his glass on the table. "Now isn't that something. This homely village: loving, neighborly, safe – all the things the big wicked city isn't — and guess what lurks under the quaint surface? Homicidal maniacs wielding needle and thread rubbing elbows with international art thieves."

"John," Gray said.

"No, you can't rob me of this fun."

"Let's hear what Vivienne has to say." He turned towards his former detective, already halfway through her wine. "How did you end up here?"

"I couldn't stay in Montreal," she said. "Not after you left and Saleem—" She took another gulp of wine. "An undercover job seemed the best alternative, and it's only coincidence that brings me to your door."

"Those two men on the yacht looked dangerous. I presume from what you've said that they're smugglers." He ran a hand through his hair. "You went out alone with them?"

"Oui. They needed an engineer, and I know almost as much about boats as you do. I volunteered for this operation."

"I'd never assign one of my officers to such a mission. I don't like it."

"Neither do I," she said. "But they're moving priceless stolen works out of the country. Halfmoon Bay is the last stop before they head east. The Far East. And as their engineer, I can poke around the boat as much as I want without suspicion."

And be thrown overboard, but he kept that thought to himself.

"Who are they?"

"Stan and Diego. Stan wears that captain's hat, but he's no captain. I'm thinking the yacht's stolen, and not reported because they took care of the owner. Diego's the less emotional one; stares at you when you're not looking.

Gray rubbed his tired eyes, needing a reprieve from the two people counting on him for answers. He let his palms linger on his face while he decided what to do.

The log in the hearth crackled, dispersing sparks and a sandalwood-like aroma into the room.

He wasn't her superior officer at the moment and couldn't order Vivienne to stop, and she wouldn't listen to him anyway.

"You can go back home to Montreal," he said. "Leave this smuggling operation to me."

Vivienne didn't reply. Whatever trauma she'd suffered in her personal life, whatever isolation, he wasn't blameless in it.

If he hadn't caught that last murderer and exposed Saleem's involvement... if Gray hadn't destroyed his family and driven Sita away... Vivienne would still be in Montreal, working in the safe cocoon of a supervised investigative team.

Instead of wrangling smugglers and killers single-handed.

Who was she trying to punish by taking on this dangerous mission? He knew from experience the spectre that egged her on, the guilt that hounded them both, wouldn't recede without some form of danger or sacrifice. Absolution was never that easy.

"His brain is computing the options," Seymour said over his drink. "And calculating how to best save this rocking ship from hitting an iceberg."

If only Seymour would shut up and let him think.

Vivienne caught his eye. "I'm going to see this through."

"What can I do to change your mind?"

"Nothing."

Art smugglers living in his town, and a picture of a painting in the murder victim's house—a murder victim who was also an art critic. Was that coincidence? Not likely.

Only one path stood before Gray. Everyone and everything depended on navigating that path successfully, even if he left tire marks on Slope's head, even if it burned bridges between him and Sita.

He must solve the Stitcher murders and help Vivienne with her case — presuming they were connected — and soon. Before Vivienne left for sea with those awful men.

He didn't want to consider the ramifications of the return of The Stitcher to Halfmoon Bay; didn't want to think where else that might lead. Too many things were suddenly at stake, but the solution was obvious.

Everything rested this side of the storm.

Gray must help solve Vivienne's case before the weather cleared — before the yacht left, with Vivienne on board. Gray suddenly felt grateful to the bad weather – a storm of all things – which had taken so much in his life away.

Seymour once again reclined in Dad's chair, crossing his large feet, just as the front door opened, letting in a gust of wind and rain.

The fire was going out; a chill tore at Gray. Dad stepped in with his cane, looking like an elderly, drowned rat.

"Don't ever make me drive that death trap of yours again," Lew James said to his son. "Exige, my ass."

Seymour practically jumped out of the older man's recliner.

"Why did you go out in this weather?" Gray said. "You're seventy."

"So what? I'm not old."

Gray reached into his jacket and pulled out the photograph.

"Dad, take a look at this." He held the picture in front of the other man's face. "Do you recognize this painting?"

Vivienne joined them and examined the old worn photograph over Lew's shoulder.

Donning glasses, he moved to the recliner and took his time examining the photo.

"I don't recognize it," Vivienne said.

Lew removed his specs. "I've never seen this painting, but I'll tell you one thing – it's very, very good."

"Worth a lot?"

"The style is reminiscent of Picasso, but the photograph is too worn and blurry for me to be certain." He handed the snapshot back to Gray. "I could determine a great deal more from the original by examining brush strokes."

Despite having no corpse, a tenuous connection now existed between Vivienne's thugs and the Stitcher killing at the body farm—and it was art. Specifically, the photograph he currently held.

"Are you going back to the boat tonight?" he asked Vivienne.

"Non. Given the weather, I have a room at the Drifter's Lodge."

Thank God Slope had managed to follow one of Gray's instructions.

"Stay here with us," Lew said.

"Thank you, Mr. James, but I can't." She turned back to Gray. "They'll suspect something if I'm not back soon. Certainement, I can't be seen with a chief inspector."

"Do you have a weapon?" he said.

"Yes, a gun."

Why did that make him feel worse?

They said their goodbyes, but it was hard to let her go. Vivienne was capable of taking care of herself, but Gray she had been part of Gray's team; his responsibility. As were Dad, Sita, Noelle … and let's face it, probably Seymour as well. If Gray lost one of them, he might lose himself.

The difficult night wasn't over. Far from it. Gray finished his drink.

Another challenge awaited.

CHAPTER FOURTEEN

GRAY SAT AT the bar while Sita rinsed a few glasses. Surreptitiously he checked his watch. Ten past ten. She'd closed the restaurant and locked the front door. The town seemed tucked in for the night. Wafts of lavender, marjoram, and thyme remained from meat and seafood entrees served at dinner. Gray's mouth watered, but he couldn't stomach a bit.

Her perpetual need for distraction while discussing an unpleasant topic had always frustrated him. How strange to be experiencing this once again. He preferred people to look him in the eye while talking, but that was not her way. Or else she wouldn't have run away.

Unbidden, Gray's mind flew back to a few months earlier. To when he'd opened his front door, expecting a date, and finding his long-lost wife standing on the porch instead.

A wife who had left three years earlier, and returned cradling a toddler in her arms.

Noelle was a dead ringer for him, with her dark, straight hair, her strong chin, and most of all, the clear-as-glass emerald eyes.

Sita had reached out and hugged him first. Her waist-long hair had felt like thick strands of silk in his hands, but her expression, the way she held herself were both foreign.

And at that moment, he'd known a numbness never before felt, along with happiness, relief, and love. But it was different.

117

Confusingly different. He'd looked at Sita with new eyes he didn't wish to possess.

She had finished washing the glasses.

"You and Noelle have to leave town," Gray said. "I received a call, threatening Dad."

"Dad, not us," she said, looking up from the steel sink. She scrubbed it ruthlessly, as though trying to wipe out Gray's face. "We're fine."

"You're my family. The killer knows that."

She threw down the sponge; it bounced and nearly hit him. "What killer? What body? You believe that spook at the body farm, don't you?"

"Please don't call her that."

"Why not? Are you protecting her?"

"Look, let's not fight. You can stay with someone I know in Vancouver, free of charge. I'll arrange everything, even your ride down there."

"In this weather? Are you trying to kill me?" Sita indicated the window where the wind had picked up, and rain slashed sideways against the fogged glass.

Outside, debris and abandoned garbage cans rolled across the road. The front door shook and rattled on its hinges. Things had deteriorated since his drive back with Seymour. She was right. He couldn't risk sending Sita and Noelle out in this. Now what?

"I used to be able to talk to you, as a friend," she said. "Now there's just this underlying fear that I feel, with everything I say; as if I can't trust your response." She picked up a glass and began drying it with a cloth. "Except I don't know if it's you or me. I don't know which one of us has changed."

"We both have."

118

"And who is this person in Vancouver I'd be staying with – free of charge? A girlfriend?"

"Don't," Gray said. All the while wondering how he was going to protect them.

Should he bring mother and daughter back to the cottage? Not with that recent threat. And he couldn't stay with them all the time with a murder to investigate.

"Reggie told me what your scientist said. She imagines dead people because that's her obsession. Sutured lips and a missing body? For God's sake. I don't see why I should have to leave my home, my place of business over her delusions."

"Reggie Slope is wrong about Emmy."

"Oh, it's Emmy now. We've moved on from Dr. Kaur, haven't we? Has your brown fever resurfaced, or is she better than me because she's half white? The missing link between us?"

He couldn't believe she'd said that. An indifference to cultural differences had always been a strength between them. How could loss change a person this much?

Gray wasn't used to Sita being jealous; that had never been a problem before. Or maybe he'd never taken the time to uncover her insecurities. Another failure, another lack on his part she was probably all too willing to point out.

Gray's head pounded. A sheen of sweat coated his aching body. He had to get through to her.

She leaned against the counter, waiting for him to respond. Her motives felt mixed, a tangled web he was caught in, and Emmy's description of the body came to mind: the strangulation marks. Unbidden, the image of his child as a future victim slammed his brain.

"Don't make this about our relationship," he said. "We can't sort that out now, not with a killer loose."

"There is no killer!"

Except maybe you, her eyes seemed to say. No matter how much she may or may not want Gray back, that thought still stood between them.

Had he ever apologized for being a workaholic? For not being there for her in so many ways? No. Should he apologize now? Of course he should.

His nostrils flared, and his fists clenched. Frustration burned a hole inside him.

"We never could talk through our problems," he said.

"Because you make too much out of things, like you have with what's happening at the body farm."

"What?"

"Craig was a naturally nervous child. He didn't need a helicopter dad. We didn't need someone constantly pointing out our faults."

"Every time I make a suggestion," Gray said, "you think I'm controlling you."

"You suggested we leave town; I said no, now that's that."

"I understand it's too late to leave in this weather." Gray held out his hands in appeal. "Noelle's life could be in danger. You want me to protect her, don't you? Only a few hundred people live in this village during the winter; those aren't great odds with a serial killer on the loose. We've found the victim's car, Sita. Even Reggie agrees something's going on."

"I'm tired of being controlled, do you understand? I have every right to be furious with you, to never forgive you. You never approved of what I thought or felt."

"That's not true."

"Nothing was perfect enough. You threw us into a pit to teach us that life is tough; we didn't make it out of that pit, Gray."

"What pit? How hard was your life?"

"Craig could never have met up to your expectations; he'd be trying to please you forever. To satisfy the Iceman father who found his family wanting because they're not perfect.

"You have to stop talking now."

Her breath came sharp and fast. "I don't want to stop. I should have screamed like this years ago. And left you. Then maybe, my son would be alive."

"Then why did you come back?"

Silence slammed between them. What the hell was he saying?

A wrench twisted in his gut. Even though he was to blame... for the life of him... he couldn't give in to bullying. He couldn't.

And wasn't this the flaw she's mentioned? His ego — expectations of himself and others — which had cost them a son.

She wasn't going to take Noelle to Vancouver; she wasn't going to stop attacking him. He had to sidestep this conflict, prevent it from turning into another festering wound. But the need to defend was too great. Even when he knew he was wrong, he had suffered that wrong in isolation for three long years.

"I didn't kill Craig. The storm killed him. I don't control the weather any more than I control whether an earthquake sinks us all into the Pacific."

"At least then I'd be with Craig."

This couldn't be happening. No way. Not like this. What the hell did she want from him? What did everyone want from him?

"I'm trying to help Noelle, keep her safe."

Don't say it, something inside him screamed; don't do this to her, but he shot out the words anyway. "It was my fault. I know. Believe it or not, I have tried to change. But you're becoming overemotional. And besides, the loss could have brought us closer together. We could have been a family if you had only—"

Sita threw a bottle at the wall. It smashed and left wine-colored shards sliding down the white surface.

Every muscle in her body stiffened; words ground out of her teeth like rounds from a machine gun.

"Noelle and I are not going anywhere. And I'm through with you telling me what to do. So, fuck off. Do you hear me, fuck off!"

CHAPTER FIFTEEN

THE DRIVE HOME passed in a blur. Gray couldn't recall making that left turn off Redrooffs Road, winding down the mud road towards the ocean, or pulling into his wide cobblestoned drive. At least the sky offered a partial if temporary reprieve from the rain.

He'd lost control since his return to Halfmoon. And he was saying things – foolish, immature things. It had to stop.

Pushing himself up from the bucket seat, Gray examined the weathered pavement stones at his feet, held together by concrete he and dad had poured when he was fifteen.

Some of the edges, now cracked from decades of use, appeared gritty and dark compared to the remainder of the red and white stone.

How simple life was in those days: Mom writing her book inside, yelling out that lemonade awaited them on the round kitchen table; her intense face hovering over the obsolete electric typewriter she refused to discard, a pencil behind one ear, an invariably ignored cup of coffee forming a thick film of skin to her right.

Before Gray's mistakes. Before Mom passed out of their lives.

Sita was right; he had changed. But revealing it might lead to what? Resolution? A return to that intimate yet tethering domesticity characteristic of family life.

Or more shamefully, one where he'd be forced to surrender the one thing which sustained him: his solitude.

Gray decided to take his nightly constitutional walk before going inside the cottage.

Since his return, through unspoken agreement, his long-time neighbors had given him that space this time of night – to walk the lonely beach, to visit the vastness of the ocean and attend the spot where it had all happened.

Other town residents didn't blame him the way Sita did. But then he'd grown up here; he was one of their own, accepted, and loved even.

They saw Gray with kind eyes and cast him in the role of co-victim, because something real had died inside Gray that terrible night. And something frightening had been born.

The raw wind cut across his face. It had begun to drizzle again, and the surface of the water glittered like molasses. Waves crashed upon the rounded, worn boulders lining the shore, with the frothy foam shooting upwards and violently back into the black depths as though pulled by an unseen hand.

To the left, dark bushes twined between towering pine, birch, and maple formed an impenetrable wall, which swayed back and forth.

Nature on both sides felt alive with movement while he stood still in between.

Turning to face the sea, he tried not to reimagine what Craig had endured. The cold. The pain. The merciless, pounding current which now wore down small, fragile bones and tore at soft, supple flesh – leaving behind what? A broken boy that his father had broken. A child alone in the infinite darkness.

Gray said his son's name. The wind ate it.

The ensuing weeks after Noelle's return had inexorably drawn him back here, to this expansive place, highlighting the intractability of life's events. Aren't we all a mystery – especially to ourselves? And did life pound on us, like wave after wave upon the rocks, to push us to solve that mystery?

His lungs felt drenched in a salty tang, making it harder to breathe.

The numbing pain in his hand returned; the scar was a dark-wine color and the middle fingers stiff and wooden. Sculpting Craig's face wouldn't bring him back. And that hardened molded image couldn't live and experience what Craig had missed.

The world momentarily blurred. He turned away and looked down the length of the beach.

A lump lying up ahead resembled Craig sleeping in his twin-sized bed, curled up in a ball with his blankets kicked off.

He had always slept that way. If only Gray could tuck his son in, one last time — as he had on those peaceful nights long ago, not knowing that some things lost never come back.

Gray's legs moved of their own volition towards the huddled figure. I'm coming, son…. it's windy and cold… I'm coming.

His thighs burned; pain shot through his head as he got closer and closer – and soon he'd reach the mirage; but it wasn't a mirage, it had to be Craig.

The form took life.

The dim light outlined a small shape with arms and legs sprawled. A child?

Gray's pulse throbbed, the frantic pounding accompanied by his labored breath, the rustling trees, and the constant thrashing of the sea.

Heat flushed every inch of his skin, scalding, burning; and then, still at a distance, he made out the dark, short hair.

The object lay in a fetal position, tan skin torn and ripped and rippling in the wind.

Except, closer now, he saw it wasn't skin. The image registered, and his knees buckled under him, and he fell onto his hands.

Sand as gritty as glass dug under his nails while the frigid surf slapped and grabbed, soaked his pants.

No. No.

He had to get closer; he must go and see. Foolish delusions always proved futile. A crippling rage surged through him.

It wasn't skin, he saw. It was something else shrouded in darkness, splaying threaded fingers from neck to hips – a coat. A woman's jacket.

Not a boy; not Craig.

Pale stockinged legs lay bent at the knees, with feet encased in low black boots. Wet sand curdled the short black hair. Red, youthful lips pulled down at the edges, unnaturally tethered.

This person wasn't his child — it was someone else's.

Gray pushed himself up and stopped, noting a sudden silence. For a moment, the wind stilled, the tide didn't ebb.

Delilah Atkinson's body blurred and cleared. He wiped his eyes and tried to focus until sanity returned.

A rush of surf came his way, but strategically located boulders formed a protective V around the body. Soon, the tide would rise above the rocks, and salt water would contaminate the scene.

After reaching into his pocket, he cursed. His phone must have dropped out in the car.

Which meant running back to the cabin to phone Slope, Seymour, and a SOCO team — before the killer removed this body; before the water destroyed everything.

It dawned on Gray that this Stitcher chose him as a witness — a chief inspector. They must be mad – or else... damned clever.

A volcano bubbled inside him. The poor girl's eyes were closed and puffy, her full lips pierced and puckered with nylon thread — all red, and blue, and distorted — just as Emmy had described... just as he had imagined — and Gray wanted nothing more than to rip the killer's heart out.

For tearing the life out of this poor young woman; for leaving the body here, for Gray to find.

The policeman inside him finally kicked in.

He must gather any observations he could and preserve whatever evidence remained — before calling for help.

The surf might wash away evidence, maybe even swallow the body, but a more immediate threat existed: Gray would bet the killer hid on the sidelines this very minute — watching, relishing — waiting to take away Delilah's dead body the second Gray left.

A few footprints led from the trees to the victim, footprints barely visible in the dry, compacted sand, and already dispersing in the raw wind.

He burned their size and shape to memory and looked all around. But there was nothing. No dropped clues, no indication of more than one person carrying the body, arranging it, and leaving.

To his left, bushes packed within densely grown trees continued to rustle. The prints stopped immediately before the woodland.

Without a flashlight, making chase after a hidden killer could prove deadly. He'd already tried that once, although one thing was now in his favor.

If only the clouds would part, he'd be able to see in the moonlight, but they hovered overhead like thick gray soaked sponges ready to plummet to earth.

How could he leave Delilah? Abandon her to the sea and sky? But he must.

Taking off his jacket, he swung it around and covered her face, knowing how futile the gesture was before turning toward the thicket once again. Gray knew this stretch of land better than anyone.

The hell with it.

He ran into the darkness.

If he couldn't see the killer, the killer couldn't see him – and any torch would surely give the culprit away.

Icy fingers tore at his clothes. His cheeks were already numb. Reaching the tree-line, he lifted each leg in turn and climbed over the alaskan willow before squeezing past the jutting needles of a western larch. Inside the protective canopy, perfumed pine replaced the ocean's tangy saltiness.

The killer could only watch from so many spots in this darkness, and must have seen Gray discover the body. Must have watched him mourn for Craig.

Red scalding heat flooded Gray's face. He tore through the brush, a canopy of dried leaves crunching under his feet. The deafening sound of crickets echoed in his skull, broken only by the pounding of his blood.

Something crunched a few meters ahead, and he whipped through the thicket.

Stopping only a moment to listen, he pushed forward some more, knowing someone crept nearby. Let them attack. Let them try, and he'd rip out their eyes and strip off their skin for threatening Dad and invading his home.

Nothing sounded nearby, and the constant pounding in his skull eased.

Gray evened his breath. Stopping, breathing in the scent of rotting leaves broken by gusts of salty wind, he re-evaluated the situation.

What the hell was he doing? Trampling all evidence near the body and in the woods where the culprit hid – further compromising the investigation.

He had to leave Delilah where she lay and accept the inevitable. The culprit would drag away the body, but in doing so, leave more evidence of their coming and going.

But another option came to mind -- one he hadn't thought to consider until now. Could he go against every trained instinct? Break every rule of detection and suffer the wrath of Slope and any future investigating officers? Would he be able to defend his actions, given that Slope wasn't yet entirely convinced of any murder having occurred?

The alternative loomed heavier. Leaving Delilah's body, so that it could be taken away by a monster, was out of the question. Teddy wouldn't be able to mourn her loss — the way Gray never got to see his son's broken body. The way Gray never got closure, and now came to this beach, forever craving completion and a way to say goodbye.

He wouldn't leave Delilah with the Stitcher.

Now, ripping through the scrub and relieved to get out of the thicket, Gray returned to the beach where the rolling surf opened before him, and the clouds hung low and heavy. Fresh air cleared his nostrils as he took in the panoramic view of nature getting ready to burst.

But it was too late. Gray had failed again.

He ran to the spot.
Delilah's body was already gone.

CHAPTER SIXTEEN

SEATED AT HIS dining room table, Gray flipped between morning headlines, all fusing into the same awful tagline: The Stitcher Returns to Halfmoon Bay.

Damn. Damn. Damn.

The news was now public.

An every-famished Seymour was hunched over the stove, preparing breakfast.

Lew's frail hand squeezed Gray's shoulder. Instead of warmth, cold penetrated the white cotton t-shirt. He pulled at the V-neck, knowing the fabric couldn't be choking him but somehow feeling that it did.

Lew's hand now shook. "Everyone knows you found the body last night?"

"Yes."

"I'm sorry you had to see her like that. With that sewing, I mean."

His father spoke to the son, not the policeman. Solving crimes hardened you, but personal involvement could ruin an investigation, and Gray's objectivity had gone out the window when someone threatened Dad's life.

What must Dad be feeling with a killer singling him out — fear, vulnerability because he couldn't defend himself against a much younger assailant?

Deep crevices traveled down Lew's nose to his chin. The cleft which had stood out so proud and masculine in Gray's childhood, now sagged and crinkled along its edges. But Lew's overall vitality defied these individual markers of age.

Seymour leaned against the fireplace to Gray's left, legs crossed, sipping his orange juice, silently watching the exchange. He pointed towards the full glass of juice, eggs, and bacon before Gray. When had he put it there?

Food was out of the question, but something other than coffee might help clear the fog in Gray's head. The last two cappuccinos hadn't made a speck of difference.

He'd been up all night with the SOCO team, and an apologetic yet defiant Slope. A few residents watched, huddled under their waterproof jackets, bracing the wind and rain. Their expressions reflected a combination of shock, pity, and something even less palatable — blame that Gray had brought another death to their beach. Their loyalty to the local boy clearly battled a wish to have him gone.

Lifting the cold glass of juice, he wiped the dripping beads of condensation with his thumb and brought the rim to his mouth. The sweet astringency brought forth a flood of saliva; cold slid down his parched throat.

The two men would choose their words carefully, give him space to regroup. Seymour, for one, would never miss a chance of being part of the action. The doctor placed his empty glass on the mantle.

"I'm not the local forensic, but I know the head of the SOCO team. He'll inform me of what they find."

"Why aren't you already involved?" Lew asked.

"When there's no actual body, there's no pathologist. That's why I can butt into the investigation without stepping on any toes. Unlike–"

"Me." Gray downed the juice and slammed the glass on the table. "Slope gets to treat me like a bloody witness now. As if controlling him wasn't difficult enough."

Seymour plumped down on the sofa. "He enjoyed patronizing you. What did he say? 'Are you alright, Inspector? It can be traumatizing coming across a body. Anyone I should call?' Honestly, James, I'd like a few moments with the sergeant in the morgue."

"I should have carried Delilah back to the cottage right away," Gray said. "Instead of searching for the killer. Losing my head, plunging into the thicket blind like that, I lost perspective."

Lew moved to the window, his cane clicking the floor. The rubber tip was asymmetrically worn. Gray would get him a new one first chance.

"You behaved like a human being," Lew said. "Not a policeman."

"I'm a policeman."

His father turned back and smiled. "Always so serious. Even as a child. We don't choose what happens to us, or the storms we must endure." His gaze drifted out the window again, past the line of trees, to the sea.

Gray knew what he must be thinking: that his grandson lay out there in the water.

Gray couldn't face that right now, and yet, it all felt connected: his family, Craig, the Stitcher... what Gray would do for all the people who relied on him, and what he couldn't offer Sita.

How would he tell her the truth? That her husband had drowned alongside her son? That a stranger emerged from the waves instead.

"Slope wasn't involved in the Stitcher investigation fifteen years ago, was he?" Lew asked. "As a young constable?"

"He joined the tail end of it."

Seymour chimed in. "Slope needs to focus on the recent killings, not waste time on something that happened ages ago. I'm sure we're looking at a copycat murder."

"Agreed," Gray said. "This killer must have a new motive, different from the first Stitcher. We can't pollute the investigation with irrelevant details from the past, or we risk following the wrong track altogether. Now, many of the town's occupants have changed in the past decade due to surging BC real estate prices. Only about a third of the original residents, like Dad and most of the people on the beach, remain, and among them, who would know enough to circulate details about the original Stitcher? Teddy, perhaps. He was a local political candidate back then."

"Who lost to someone more capable," Lew added. "Anything Theodore knew about the Stitcher, or any local scandal, is public knowledge, I guarantee that. Never was discreet, even back in school."

"And yet he'd hidden the fact that Delilah was her grandfather's heir."

"Not from people like me; although, he never admitted it. We all knew the old man would leave Teddy high and dry. That fault rested with old Stanley Atkinson, I think. Teddy's an okay man now, not wild like he was, but the old coot couldn't forgive his leather-jacketed, biker son, even when that son agreed to finally carry family responsibilities. If Teddy hadn't adopted Delilah, I bet the whole estate would've gone to cancer research or something. Hell, maybe that would've been better."

"Better than Farrah Stone getting her hands on the money?" Seymour asked.

Lew snorted. He seemed to think that sufficed as a response.

"Fifteen years of police experience tells me this is no maniacal killer," Gray said. "There's reason and purpose to these crimes. They're planned and executed efficiently and reproduced accurately: that's not the result of an out-of-control person. It indicates discipline."

"But doesn't exclude hate," Seymour said. "I agree there's a purpose behind these crimes, but what sort of crazy bugger strangles, mutilates, and then steals bodies? What sense does that make?"

"That's the key, isn't it?" Lew said, moving towards them. "Find out why the killer took the bodies, and I'll bet you'll solve the crime."

Perhaps Gray had inherited his detection skills from Dad's razor-sharp mind.

"How long was Slope secretly engaged to Delilah? Why would she choose him?"

His father took his time getting to the sofa. "That's an interesting question. Makes you not quite trust our local dick, doesn't it?"

"What do you mean?" Seymour asked. "Was he marrying for money?"

"What else?" Lew said. "You think that shark loved anyone, ever? Even his own mother, rest her soul? She died alone in an old-folks home twenty miles from here, did you know that?"

Gray shook his head.

"Yeah. I saw Slope's mom as often as I could. She called out for her son in those last moments, but he was too busy having dinner with Teddy and Delilah. None of the three cared for Mona one bit, and she raised that boy singlehanded, working at the local grocers during the day, the motel some nights. It isn't easy making ends meet in this town, not since so much of foreign investment bought up our West Coast. I don't know how she survived as a single mom."

Gray rose and began making cappuccinos. Maybe more caffeine would clear his sleep-deprived brain. "Slope seemed affected by Delilah's death, but also acted as though he didn't believe me."

"Acted is right, son. He can't lead that investigation now, not with his involvement with Delilah."

Seymour said, "Gray can't lead the investigation either."

Lew sighed. "No, he can't."

"Slope kept the engagement under wraps for a reason. What did Teddy think of it?"

"Theodore Atkins understands compromise, like most of my generation. We fought for what we've got in this world. Know when to retreat. Delilah was what we might still refer to as a 'loose woman,' and Slope's probably better than some of the trash she's brought home."

Gray brought over the coffees, but the older man shook his head.

Lew reached for his cane and pushed himself up. A frail man in body if not spirit, he reminded Gray of the passage of time – that Gray would one day be old and alone too, possibly in this very town.

"One more thing." Lew turned at his bedroom door. "Don't trust Slope with evidence. I never liked that boy; he lied to me plenty over the years."

With that, he retired to his room. The previous sleepless night must be costing Dad more than it cost him or Seymour.

A pounding on the door made Gray turn. What now?

"I'll get it," Seymour said.

He opened the door a crack, and through the flashes and torrent of speech, Gray realized a second surge from the press was upon him. Seymour seemed to enjoy the attention, delivered the phrase 'no comment' repeatedly, and firmly shut the door.

"Are you certain SOCO found nothing on the beach?" Gray said.

"I told you – between wind, rain, and all that trampling you did, nothing of value. The footprint you saw was washed away by the time we arrived. Covering the area with your jacket was a good idea, but it couldn't prevent the tide from sweeping in."

"What about the ground among the trees?"

"Now, let me see. Size eleven shoes –" Seymour pointed at Gray's bare feet. "— trampled all the wild grass, flowers, and foliage." He stopped smiling. "What the hell were you thinking?"

Gray held up both hands. "I know, I know. I messed up. Some green police cadet would have done better."

"A girl guide would have done better, James."

Gray gulped down the cappuccino, wiping the foam from his lips. "I felt rage, pure and simple."

"Very professional."

"I'm not you, Doctor."

Seymour huffed. "Thank heavens for that. Or we'd both be bored to death."

Gray pushed himself up. He grabbed his cup with his bad hand, and it spilled.

Out of the corner of his eye, he saw Seymour's head shake, so slightly that he might have imagined it. Gray took the cup to the sink.

"You know why the killer chose me to find Delilah's body?"

"Why?" Seymour asked.

"So I couldn't take over to officially investigate. I'm cast as a witness now. This Stitcher is smart as well as ruthless."

Seymour fell into a nearby chair. "I hadn't thought of that."

"Slope, I can control. Let's hope the constabulary doesn't send a third detective to take over."

That would likely happen after the bad weather passed. Gray didn't say it, didn't want to explain, but the only safe passage was to solve the killings now — in the eye of the storm.

CHAPTER SEVENTEEN

EMMY STEPPED OUT of the pickup into the misty air and slammed the heavy door. 28 Beaver Road looked renovated, unlike most of the tightly sandwiched dwellings encircling the small lake. A few steps led down to a small pebbled beach, and wafts from rotting fish drifted upward. On a normal day, the lake would be calm, but today, the surface of the water rippled, and a floating dock secured by barrels on all four sides pounded back and forth upon the surface.

A streetlamp threw a pale phosphorescence over the paved road. Why had Emmy come here? What did she expect to accomplish going over Slope and Gray James's heads?

A certain vindication, perhaps? She didn't appreciate the sergeant's condescending attitude, or the Chief Inspector's interrogations. Emmy deserved neither. All she'd come here to do was conduct her research and make a modest life for herself. Where she'd failed in the city, she had hoped to succeed in a less demanding environment — and what had happened? The local women hate her, and some bloody maniac leaves a mutilated corpse on her land.

Or more specifically, Teddy's land.

Farrah must have plenty of influence over her aging fiancé, especially in the sexual department. No sixty-year-old man would trade in a younger, hot-to-trot woman for the satisfaction of forensic research. Emmy had no illusions about how far Teddy's respect for her would stretch in a tug-of-war with Farrah.

A light switched on in the ground floor salon of the house.

Emmy checked her watch: only 7:30 am. Would Mrs. Franklin mind so early a visit, given their appointment wasn't until 9 am?

The thought of killing an hour and a half in the local downtown café (owned by Sita, and frequented by many of the people at yesterday's protest) didn't sound appealing.

After climbing the three cement steps as slowly as humanly possible, Emmy knocked on the maroon-colored door.

The entrance hall light was on, and a vaguely-lineated shadow looked through the frosted glass of the front door. It opened to reveal a tall and lithe woman in her seventies (who looked like she still religiously performed all her Jane Fonda workouts) opened the door. She even looked like the actress, and didn't appear surprised by the early call. Maybe she had heard the truck pull up at the front of the house.

"You're very early," a deep, confident voice said.

"I know, I'm sorry. I couldn't wait to speak to you."

Mrs. Franklin handed over the morning paper. "Follow me."

The headline made Emmy blink:

'The Stitcher returns!'

According to the story, local boy and now Chief Inspector, Gray James, had found a body late last night, but the corpse had subsequently disappeared.

"Sit and read it, dear," Mrs. Franklin said.

Emmy mindlessly took the chair closest to her at the kitchen table, her eyes glued to the page.

The story went on to explain the previous night's events in glorified detail: how Gray, since everyone in town knew him by his first name, had found the body around 11 pm — a strangled girl whose lips had been sutured shut with surgical nylon, just like fifteen years ago, the reporter said. Gray chased the killer but lost him, then returned to the beach; but the deal girl was gone.

Mrs. Franklin's eyes were on Emmy the entire time she was reading; narrowed, assessing.

"I suppose people will believe me, now," Emmy said.

"I suppose so. Not everyone remembers the first crime. Most of the residents are new; the older folks have moved away or died off. Local real estate agents make a point of not mentioning the Stitcher killing to Vancouverites looking to buy coastal shacks. They'll all know now, the young and the old, the minute they have their morning coffee. And everyone will be discussing it."

"This time it was a girl."

"You found a dead man, correct?" Mrs. Franklin said. "Like the first time, all those years ago."

Her eyes lowered. It must be painful, even after all this time? Emmy never was good at condolences.

"Don't let me stop you," Mrs. Franklin continued. "The article gets better. Gray James, of course, identified the victim."

Delilah Chen Atkinson.

Oh my God, Emmy though. Poor Teddy. Poor Delilah; not that she'd met the adopted daughter more than once or twice. Her impression was of a lost girl, immersing herself in a vulgar rather than satisfying sexuality.

She blinked, remembering what Teddy had said: that Delilah liked Slope. Teddy feared an impending announcement — one which he loathed for multiple reasons.

141

He'd once vented about Slope's possibly marrying into the family, getting his hands on Teddy's various properties.

But how could Slope have done that with Teddy and Farrah alive? Unless Delilah owned some of the property herself. What the hell did that mean for Emmy's farm?

"It's quite a coincidence," Mrs. Franklin said, fracturing Emmy's thoughts. "Another Stitcher killing, just before you visit me to discuss the first."

"That's true. I only wanted to clear my reputation, prove I hadn't hallucinated the entire thing. People hate me in this town as it is. Now, maybe people will believe me."

"But at what cost?" the older woman said. "Another victim's life. A young woman's."

Emmy should have added that. "Of course. Poor, unfortunate Delilah."

"She was a slut, my dear. Not unlike her soon-to-be stepmother."

Seeing Emmy's shocked expression, she added, "I call them as I see them. When you're my age, and everyone around you is either gone or senile, you don't beat around the bush." Then she winked. She actually winked.

Emmy cleared her throat and put down the paper before plunging ahead with her mission.

"I don't disagree with you, Mrs. Franklin. Farrah Stone and her friends —"

"We call them her "Angels," dear."

"Yes, she and her Angels have made running the farm more difficult. I might even lose that land if Teddy gives in to her."

"It's unfortunate then that Delilah is probably dead. You could have discussed the farm with her."

Emmy lost her train of thought. "What? You mean Delilah owns... I mean, owned, the farm?"

"I'm almost Teddy's contemporary." She patted her hair. "Give or take a few years. His father's low opinion of him was common knowledge. If Delilah got away with murder in that house, it was because her grandfather adored her."

"And left her the mansion?"

"Perhaps. Let's not get sidetracked. You've come to discuss the first Stitcher victim, fifteen years ago. My husband, Ronald." She rose and moved to the kitchen "First, let's get you some coffee. You're as pale as a ghost."

"I always look like that."

"They say time heals all wounds, but in this case, there were none to heal. The Stitcher, God bless him, whoever he was, did me an incredible favor. I was thrilled. Ronald was a bastard, and I've never been happier than after his death. Honestly, it was like winning the lottery."

She returned with the French press and poured a dark sludge-like brew into two white mugs. Emmy's had a lily on it, and Mrs. Franklin's had a picture of a wrestler Emmy didn't recognize.

"Your husband was strangled with his lips sutured? Like the body I found?"

"Yes, that must have been awful for you."

"And there were no clues as to who killed him?" Emmy asked. "Police never found out who did it?

The old woman shook her head slowly as she sipped, clearly unperturbed that the killing had gone unsolved.

"It's a mystery to this day," she said. "Sergeant Slope's boss—now what was his name?—investigated. No fingerprints, no suspects. That inspector was a good man, thoroughly competent. If he couldn't find the culprit, the killer must have left town and never come back.

"Until now," Emmy said.

Mrs. Franklin chuckled. "Certainly not. That person is long gone, maybe even dead. I don't think you should be looking at that old case."

The older woman looked thoughtful, perhaps even secretive. Her long and wrinkled fingers rested on an elegant, strong chin; her thin lips were relaxed and not at risk of divulging anything their owner preferred kept private.

Perhaps Mrs. Franklin liked to have the upper hand, or maybe she merely wanted to project that appearance. If she knew something, did that mean she might know the original Stitcher's identity? Did the killer still live in this town, walk among the residents with a clear conscience like a wolf in sheep's clothing?

If that were the case, the older woman's life might be in danger.

Emmy brought a hand to her forehead.

"What is it?" Mrs. Franklin asked.

She didn't wish to be the only one responsible for the older woman's safety. She needed to talk to Seymour or Slope.

But could Slope be trusted?

Anyone could have committed that murder fifteen years ago – with the exception of younger people such as Matisse and Delilah.

Poor Delilah.

The coffee tasted chocolatey, despite resembling coarse brown mud. Fortunately, it had its intended effect.

"Are you alright, dear?"

"No, actually, I'm not. I wish I could run away."

The other woman's eyes softened. She placed a lined hand over Emmy's.

"Why don't you? Run far away from this place and never come back."

What did she mean by that?

"You've gone awfully quiet," Mrs. Franklin said.

Emmy was direct if nothing else. "Do you know who killed your husband?"

Mrs. Franklin finished her coffee, the wrestler's bloated face streaked by dripping brown liquid.

"No. I don't. But I'll say one thing — what's done, is done. No use rattling old skeletons."

"Your life could be in danger."

"What? After all these years? If I knew the killer's identity — which I don't — why am I not already dead?"

I don't know, Emmy thought. You're mysterious and gutsy, and I like you.

"And why has the killer not used those medical instruments on me?" Mrs. Franklin added. "Those things the Stitcher left beside Ronald's body."

"What?"

A tree branch scraped against the window. Outside, the wind howled.

"The police found the suture needle and medical instruments used on Ronald at the crime scene, next to his body." Mrs. Franklin rested her chin in her hand and wore a Mona Lisa smile. "You must have seen them, Emmy. Weren't they next to your corpse as well?"

CHAPTER EIGHTEEN

SEYMOUR COULD DETECT the burning toast from the street, wafts drifting forward from the open kitchen window of number 21 Caldwood – a humble bungalow on the crescented cul-de-sac just off Redrooffs Road. Gray had sent him to get the email Slope was slow to hand over – the one posted by the missing babysitter who could be the Stitcher's first victim. The Virtue family was indulging in a late and dubious breakfast.

The small and dilapidated cottage looked in need of TLC. His knock on the door resulted in a jerky opening, loud shrieking, and an assault of smoke.

"Yes?" A weary-eyed woman stood slouching before him. Her hair was perfectly groomed to match the burgundy business suit she wore, although the latter screamed mass-market. "Calen's watching TV, and I'm in a rush to leave for Vancouver for a board meeting." She yelled out for her husband. "Steve!"

"I'm Dr. Seymour. I called and spoke to your husband."

Mrs. Virtue stepped aside and let him in.

"Come in." She sounded surly to Seymour's mind. If she needed reminding of his official capacity, his forensic pathologist identification burned inside his coat pocket. That would trump her alleged board meeting.

Bringing a hand to his midriff, Seymour steadied the grumbling in his stomach. The morning's single egg was long ago digested.

He planned to hold out for a proper meal, loathe to lower himself to consume an unpalatable congealed offering of overcooked eggs and Joan of Arc bread, should food be offered in the first place. A cup of coffee might hit the spot, though — unless, of course, they offered him instant.

A burly Steve Virtue came out of the living room, where a child sat watching cartoons. The father's right eye twitched, and he wore sweats, stained on the thighs from many a meal before the TV. Seymour had trouble trusting a man who reminded him of Edward G. Robinson's villainous character in the film *Key Largo*. Bogart should never have trusted him either.

"Let's go into the kitchen," he said, in a higher voice than Seymour would have expected, before addressing his wife. "Sue, join us."

She hesitated. "I'll stay a minute, but no more."

Dirty dishes filled the kitchen sink, counter, and even a corner of the floor. The smoky stink was worst here, but apparently the seven-year-old's cartoons couldn't be interrupted, and the kitchen was the only available space for their discussion.

Seymour would never understand modern parents. No wonder the world was going to hell.

The other man was holding out a sticky table chair. "Sit down. How can we help?"

Jam adorned the offered seat. Seymour took another.

"Thank you for meeting with me. Chief Inspector James and I are with the Vancouver Homicide Division, and although we have no official jurisdiction here," he held out both palms in

147

benevolent intent, "information about your babysitter could help us in another investigation."

Sue stood clutching her coat to her chest. Steve's eyes narrowed.

"You're talking about Calen's claim he found his babysitter in the backyard, strangled and stitched at the lips? It's crap, eh. He tells a lot of lies these days."

"I believe him," Sue said, a little too quickly. Her eyes shot darts at her husband. "He doesn't lie about the important things, only about buying gummy bears at the variety store, and there's the odd day he skips school. But like I say to the teacher, he's only a kid, and this isn't grad school, you know."

Seymour, who recalled skipping afternoon classes for a month until his elementary school teacher threatened to inform his father, couldn't have agreed more.

Steve closed his eyes and spoke in a mock-tolerant tone which even Seymour knew, from his limited success with women, was unwarranted.

"Getting hysterical won't help him behave. He's a boy, and boys need a firm hand."

Sue's grip tightened around her coat. Had she ever been at the receiving end of that firm hand?

Given Steve's casual attire and lack of hurry to get anywhere, it appeared she pulled double duty as both provider and caregiver. No one could be missing the babysitter more than her.

Joanie Skolowski was a London resident, in BC temporarily for work. She'd worked for the Virtues for precisely six months before leaving unexpectedly.

"Where did Calen find her?" Seymour said.

Steve grabbed a piece of burnt toast and sat opposite Seymour. He began spreading soft butter across the charcoal surface, before reinserting the gritty knife into the brick of butter.

"Through those trees on the right side of our yard, next to the fence." He held up his hand, and a ring on his third finger, caught the light.

"You can't see it from here, or else we'd have looked out the window when he screamed. By the time he came in, pulled on my shirt a few times, got me away from the hockey game – the Vancouver Canucks beat Toronto, by the way – a few minutes passed. Two at the most. I got on my shoes, let him yank me to the spot, and nothing. In my day, I'd get smacked for a stunt like that."

Sue's eyes met Seymour's; her lower lip trembled.

Her husband chewed his toast with his mouth open.

"Turns out, Joanie went back home," Steve said. "I got an email from her the next day when she landed in London, eh, sayin' she was sorry and all that. I swear, those Brits have no work ethic. I mean, Sue kills herself commuting between Vancouver and here three times a week. How's she supposed to take care of the brat, too?"

Seymour stood, unable to stomach any more. "Can I have a copy of that email?"

"I gave it to Slope."

"I know. It's easier if I get a copy now instead of troubling Sergeant Slope. He's occupied with protests at the body farm."

Steve's eyes lit up. "That place. Talk about ghouls doing whatever they do in the name of science. No wonder my kid's confused and seeing corpses."

Seymour brought the man back on topic. "Your son saw the body on the twenty-second of September?"

"Yeah, maybe."

"What time was that?"

149

"The game started at seven. So maybe around eight."

And you allowed your small child to wander in the dark outside, unattended, at seven pm, Seymour thought. The killer could have been nearby. The killer could have attacked Calen.

Sue's curt, "I'm leaving now," indicated she shared Seymour's sentiment. He followed her to the door while Steve printed out a copy of the babysitter's email.

"Mrs. Virtue," Seymour said. "You said you believe your son. You believe Joanie is dead."

She looked nervously towards the home office, where a printer sounded. Why would she be frightened of Steve Virtue? But Seymour had long ago given up on understanding the skewed dynamics of dysfunctional marriages. He felt grateful to have escaped being tangled and suffocated in that particular fisherman's net himself.

She finally answered. "Yes, I believe she's dead."

"Why does your husband disagree?"

"How do I know? If he were a man, I'd divorce him."

Email in hand, and content with his work, Seymour left the Virtue house, wondering is Sue realized she was quoting Christie, and also conscious of the fact that no one had bothered to offer him that cup of coffee.

CHAPTER NINETEEN

PINE COVE MANSION loomed overhead as rain crashed to earth from above.

The front steps were a good thirty yards from the driveway, and Emmy sidestepped the pooling puddles deftly, as though maneuvering through obstacles for some race show audition tape.

The control top hose she wore might as well be chopping her in half, but you couldn't wear a fancy dress without nylons, could you? And she didn't want to stand out.

Still, the sizeable rose-shaped taffeta bow below her cleavage must be a new fashion trend, or else the saleslady wouldn't have recommended it.

This purple, fluffy dress made her feel as stupid as a thirty-something chaperone at a prom. But what did it matter how she looked, so long as she was away from the farm and the possibility of the Stitcher returning a second time?

There were other reasons for staying at Teddy's mansion. In Emmy's absence, Farrah might talk him into closing the forensic facility.

Everything must hang together long enough for the publication of the primary results. With recognition from the University under her belt, Emmy could continue her research elsewhere, with or without Teddy as a benefactor. A few more months... all she needed were a few more months.

The Atkinson mansion invariably filled her with awe. She couldn't imagine managing a place this huge, hiring cooks, cleaners, maintenance specialists, gardeners. Of course, Butch, their manager, took care of most things, and where he lapsed, Farrah stepped in.

Emmy's hesitant knock on the carved double doors brought an immediate response. She flew back, almost falling down the porch before catching herself.

"Whoa," Teddy said, grabbing her by the arm. "Come on in, tiger."

Pulling back her shoulders, she followed him into the paneled foyer.

A curved banister to her left led to the second floor, and a grand salon was visible through an archway to her right.

The sudden contrast between outside air and the warmth from a nearby hearth heated her lungs, made her breath catch. Teddy's hand remained on her arm, and his smile conveyed that he understood her discomfiture.

"You look nice tonight, Emmy," he said.

Here he was thinking about her after the awful news of Delilah. "Are you alright, Teddy?"

He nodded. "I'm hanging in. That's why it's so good to have everyone over. I don't wanna be alone, you understand?"

She didn't, but kept the thought to herself. Extroverts confused her. They seemed to inhabit a different planet entirely.

Or else, Teddy didn't believe Delilah was dead. Now why should he question a chief inspector's first-hand report?

He patted her shoulder as though she were a pet recently rescued from a shelter. "Don't let anyone here intimidate you. You out-think and outclass the whole lot of 'em."

Did his fair Farrah count in that assessment? Best not to ask.

"Thank you. Ah, about the protest –"

"Not now, darlin'. We'll talk about that later. I'm the host tonight, and I'm gonna do a good job if it kills me. Where's your weekend bag?"

"I forgot to bring one. I was in such a rush that I didn't think straight." She'd been nervous about coming here and didn't add that a weekend with his fiancé might give her a stroke.

Teddy tilted his head and led her through the foyer. "Go get 'em, darlin. I'll send Butch over to the cottage to get a couple of your things."

A pulse jumped in her neck. "No."

"No choice. He can get you a pair of jeans, maybe a shirt. You can't sit at the breakfast table lookin' like a puff-pastry, can you?"

Butch going through her things? Emmy might have a stroke anyway.

The bloody dress shoes dug further into her skin as they walked; clumpy mascara hastily applied seemed to glue her lashes together. She used two fingers to spring them apart.

Hopefully, she'd be offered a drink soon: champagne, beer, wine from a box — anything.

As if by telepathy, Teddy pressed a glass of something bubbly into her left hand. "You'll need this before facing the group in the salon."

It burned her mouth and throat, a little tart, slightly bitter; she felt light-headed.

Before letting Teddy resume his formal duties, she said, "I spoke with Mrs. Franklin."

He nodded. "About the old murder. She wasn't too broken up, I bet. Old Franklin was a brute to her and that daughter of his—what was her name? Anyway, she moved away a long time ago. I'll tell you more about that over dinner. You know, the James family knew them all well –"

"What?"

They'd reached the salon—a formal room twice the size of here entire cottage.

"What the hell are you wearing?" Farrah stood leaning against an upholstered chair in the entry, appearing elegantly bored. "You look like Snow White covered in dwarf vomit."

Her long, painted fingers tapped the skin revealed under the thigh-high slit of her golden dress, a high-necked, sleeveless number that had a pear-shaped cut-out just above her cleavage. It may as well have been painted over her model-thin figure — so at odds with Emmy's curves.

If gaining Teddy's trust came down to feminine persuasion, how could she ever hope to compete with this mercenary Bond-girl?

Teddy spoke with Sergeant Slope at the other side of the crowded room of perfumed bodies and fake smiles; Emmy wracked her brain for a comeback but found none.

"Ah, thank you for inviting me to your house."

"I see we're ignoring your stupid outbursts at the gallery. Don't count on my generosity. I'd throw you out of this house, my land, and my town in a minute. Teddy may believe all your science crap now, but he won't when I'm through with him. Count on it."

She pivoted on one hip and slithered to the back of the room, where Sita James stood nursing a glass of red wine.

At least her green silk dress left something to the imagination. Emmy couldn't mistake the scowl directed at her by the Chief Inspector's wife. Was he also nearby, ready to renew his attack? She downed the rest of her champagne.

Rain slid down the expansive paned windows overlooking the acres of manicured lawn beyond.

Across the green, at the far back under an incline of Douglas fir and pine, a guest house resembling a brown smudged blob jutted out of the ground.

Farrah used it as a painting studio, Emmy knew, and an adjacent shed held all the tools belonging to Butch: shovels, machinery, chemicals — items he used to manage the property.

The mansion sat perched above Pine Cove. To the left of the lawn, the distant white-tipped peaks of the Pacific thrashed against a shallow cliff of rocks. Dense forest ran inland for miles to the right.

Emmy had once ventured inside during one of Teddy's cocktail parties—into the dark and mysterious woods—only to find the roar of the ocean muffled, the air surprisingly thick and still. Her heart had beaten fast; her brow had dripped with sweat. She'd run out of the thicket and across the lawn to the edge of the blowing Pacific, grateful for the misty air in her lungs and the breeze through her hair and wondering if the surf had ever risen high enough to flood the grounds and house.

Slope stood in the middle of the room and gave her a curt "hey" before proceeding to ignore her. Farrah and Sita plotted in a corner, occasionally giving Emmy a pitying look, interspersed with giggles.

All in all, it had been a fun-filled evening—one which made Emmy want to jump into the bubbling, violent waters of the cove.

No Gray James or Seymour, but Lew sat on the couch speaking to an older couple Emmy didn't recognize.

155

Farrah's son, Matisse, sat hunched in a check-patterned wing chair, staring down at the Persian at his feet. Every so often, he'd straighten out the carpet's strings messed up by passing feet.

She understood his need for action, anything to distract from social awkwardness. Here was a comrade in arms. She moved towards him.

"Where did you get the cola?" she said.

Matisse looked up. "On the sideboard, hidden behind all the booze. Mom put it there in case any of her stupid friends want a rum and coke. Here, take my chair, and I'll get you one."

A minute later, he placed a glass before her. It tasted funny, and his eyes—matching his fox-like face—watched as she took the first sip before they glanced down at the taffeta bow.

"Tastes great," Emmy lied. He seemed to relax and sat on the chaise opposite.

Matisse didn't speak while she finished the drink, but before she could place the glass on the side table, he'd taken it. Within thirty seconds he returned with a refill.

Such a gracious host. If only his mother had a tenth the warmth.

"You're a virgin, aren't you?" he said.

Emmy swallowed the wrong way and coughed. Recovering, she said:

"Excuse me?"

He raised and lowered his eyebrows. The boy was what? Nineteen? A grown man, by some accounts. Served her right for being kind.

Emmy tried to stand, but the room tilted. Falling back down, she gripped the edges of the chair and felt his shifty eyes on her once again. How could she ever have mistaken him for a comrade?

A masculine hand reached towards her, and she pulled back. The tall and dark figure hovered, and sparkling emeralds for eyes glittered, shifting between her and Matisse, assessing.

His lips pressed into a grim line, but the lower lip remained surprisingly full. Meanwhile, Matisse quickly skirted across the room like a frightened deer.

"I feel nauseous," Emmy said. The room tilted. She clutched at her chest.

"You need some food," the baritone voice replied.

It felt like seconds before he returned with a plate full of cold shrimp, sushi, and seeded crackers with Brie. Didn't Farrah serve any real food?

Emmy shoved it down and felt a fraction better, but a steady pounding began in her head.

"Don't get up for a while," Gray James said, in that smoldering way of his, looking better in his tux than chocolate cheesecake with cream on top. "You've had one too many."

"Teddy gave me a glass of champagne, and Matisse brought me some soda."

Gray picked up her empty glass and sniffed it. "I bet he did." He scanned the room with a scowl. "Trust me; you're missing nothing sitting this party out. We'll go in to dinner soon."

She hadn't noticed the dimple on his chin before. The urge to lift a finger and probe it proved irresistible, and she must have done it because he tucked her right hand back safely onto her lap.

His lightly tanned face had just the right amount of weathering, the fashionably-cut short hair in perfect keeping with the modern tux. Never before had Emmy been so fascinated with a face.

"I'll check on you later," he said, moving away in a smooth gait which highlighted each firm and rounded gluteal muscle in action.

What was happening to her? She shook her head.

Something important had been mentioned in her presence recently. But the thread kept slipping away.

Seymour stood next to Lew. He must have arrived with the Chief Inspector.

Her wobbly feet made it across the slippery tiles. Seymour saw her coming and held out a hand while wearing his usual wry expression.

"You look fantastic," he said. "Though, a little—hmmm. How much did you have to drink?"

"Only a glass of champagne when I got here. And two colas."

"Ah, my kind of woman. The kind who can't hold her liquor."

Lew rolled his eyes. "It's true what they say—youth is wasted on the young. Leave her alone, John, and go look after my son. Who knows what trouble he's getting himself into."

The elder James smelled of oak and musk, reminding Emmy of the last time she'd seen her grandfather, when she was ten. The visceral memory came so strongly, she had to blink away tears.

"Here, use my handkerchief. Only old farts like me carry them, but that one's fresh out of the laundry."

Emmy dabbed the corner of her eyes and spent the next twenty minutes in surprisingly easy conversation with Lew James. As an academic (albeit in the arts) he shared some of her sensibilities, unlike the other Neanderthals occupying this claustrophobic village.

"Wish we could get some fresh air," he said. "The gale would blow us both into the ocean."

Now she registered the backdrop of groaning wind. The glass windows jarred in their frames, ready to burst.

High-pitched voices battled the clinking of crystal and porcelain in the overheated room.

She must have been sobering up, and yet the surrounding sounds grew increasingly loud, and the slashing of rain on windowpanes pounded her ears.

"I have to get out of here. I can't stay here overnight."

"Not safe out there anymore," Lew said. "I'm staying, and so is Gray. He's not the social type, but a certain lady is also an overnight guest." He motioned towards Sita, who was engaged in ardent conversation with Gray James.

She saw Emmy and scowled. It felt like a slap.

"I have to talk to Teddy," Emmy said. Her voice sounded surer now, less distant and shaken. She was sobering up. No more bloody champagne. "That's why I came to this party—to discuss the future of my work. The University has no other facilities appropriate for this kind of research. And most of what makes my findings unique is the proximity to the Pacific, studying the unique effects this type of weather has on forensic results."

Lew nodded. He understood—what a refreshing change. He didn't argue back, or contradict her, or tell her she was a ghoul.

"I remember when I was working on my Ph.D.—" he said.

"I already have my Ph.D., Dr. James."

"Of course, you do. I meant that the art world has its share of critics too. If you take my advice, don't speak with Teddy about the farm tonight. Catch him when he's alone, maybe during coffee or a walk tomorrow morning."

159

Lew glanced out the large glass windows again; his eyes narrowed, sharp, thick lines running along the sides of his mouth. "If nature cooperates."

"Are you worried about your cottage in the storm? It's next to the beach, isn't it?"

"Yeah, but Gray took care of all that, locked it down for a couple of days. The whole coastline's on guard, even though we're only catching the bottom edge of Hurricane Mabel. Vancouver's supposed to get the worst of it."

"I'm surprised you're at a party," Emmy said. "After your son discovered Delilah's body on the beach. News of the Stitcher returning is all over town."

"The Stitcher," Lew said, eyes shooting out at hers. "What do you know about that?"

"Nothing, other than what Teddy told me. The old case is unsolved. It makes my blood boil that Slope didn't take me seriously when I found a body. He let all that evidence wash away."

"Slope's no fool. Gray came here tonight because I received a death threat, probably from the killer."

"What? What did the killer say?"

"Oh, the usual. He would stitch me up, blah, blah, blah. I'm not too fast on my feet these days. Can't outrun a killer." He thumped his nearby cane for effect. "Gray will take care of me, and keep his wife and daughter safe, too."

Here, he gave Emmy a meaningful look she couldn't comprehend.

"Where is your granddaughter?" she asked.

"Noelle's upstairs, asleep, tended by one of Teddy's staff. She's no trouble. Unlike —"

He stopped himself and pressed his lips together. His eyes shone.

"Did I say something wrong?" Emmy said. "I often do."

"No, my dear. Come, everyone's heading into dinner."

They left together.

A long, mission-style table dominated the formal dining room. The setting reminded Emmy of black and white mysteries she'd stay up late to watch on TV.

William Powell from The Thin Man movies would be sitting at the head of the table of suspects, ready to divulge the identity of the murderer...

She shook her head as a server placed asparagus and steak on her dinner plate.

The multitude of courses made Emmy's head spin, with Farrah touching none of them, and instead finding any excuse to paw Gray James—in contrast to Seymour, on Emmy's left, who enthusiastically ate every speck of food placed before him and chatted incessantly.

"You're hardly eating," he said.

"I'm not very hungry."

"Well I have to keep up my strength. I think I'm coming down with something." He cleared his throat. "You know I've been surrounded by children left right and center since I got here."

He recounted his meeting with Sue Virtue's family before spreading his wisdom to others around him.

Gray sat on Emmy's right. Once or twice, his hand grazed hers, and the resultant electrical shock made her face flame.

He'd invited her to call him Gray. Of course, that meant he could call her Emmy. Well, la dee da. Thanks a million, Inspector, for that kind gesture of informality.

"How are you?" Gray asked.

"I should be asking you that, since you found Delilah's body."

He cut his steak and took a bite, washing it down with a gulp of red wine. "The Stitcher killings have everyone tense."

"Not everyone. I went to see Mrs. Franklin regarding her husband's murder, fifteen years ago."

His classically handsome profile remained serene.

She fiddled with her sautéed vegetables, aiming for a similar casualness. "Mrs. Franklin spoke of her husband's murder, almost implied that he deserved it. Do you know anything about that?"

"Before my time."

"You'd joined the force by then. It was only fifteen years ago.'

Gray put down his cutlery with a clang. "I hadn't made detective yet. It wasn't my case."

And then Emmy remembered what had been nagging at her all evening. Something Teddy had said.

"Your family knew the Franklins," she said.

"Everyone knows Dad around here."

Across the table, Sita watched and twisted her cloth napkin. The black *kajal* outlining her large eyes seemed to jump off her face, the ruby-red lips bloodthirsty.

The waiter refilled Emmy's water glass. She sipped it before replying. "How well did you know them?"

Gray's hand paused before the wine glass reached his lips.

"I'll speak to Teddy again," Emmy said. "And find out everything."

"You're certainly thorough." He clicked her glass with his before turning his attention to the lady on his right.

Across the table, Matisse glanced from Emmy to Farrah. He exuded a mixture of hostility and admiration for his mother. Catching the boy's unguarded look, Emmy realized he saw her with similar contempt.

How awful to inadvertently witness what lay inside a stranger's heart, what they held apart from the outside world.

The filet mignon might have been excellent or made of rubber, Emmy couldn't tell.

All she wanted was to go to her assigned room, sleep through the night, muster through breakfast, and return to her isolated cabin.

There, she'd lock the doors, shut the windows, and crawl into bed and relax.

Dinner finally ended. After-dinner drinks in the library proved even less comfortable, and carried an air of expectant strain.

Gray and Seymour were elsewhere in the mansion. Only a few of the guests, the ones who planned to stay overnight, remained in the house — including Sita, Slope, and a couple of others Emmy didn't recognize.

One of the women, Sophie, addressed Farrah: "Darling, that dress is fabulous. And the makeup—" She arched a brow. "Weren't you a makeup artist in the old days, before Teddy and all this?"

Farrah smiled and waved a hand in disinterest. She caressed her pearl choker and pointed towards Emmy.

"At least I know how to make myself presentable."

"Farrah—" Teddy's jowls seemed to hang down lower than ever.

Lew joined Emmy on the sofa, and together they helplessly witnessed Farrah's assault on Matisse.

"Why are you still here, instead of upstairs in your room?" she said. "Honestly, darling – you can't follow me around like an adoring puppy forever. Go, make friends. Live your own life." She said to Sita, "Grown children are such a bore; trust me, you'll find out."

Matisse turned a combination of orange and red. The color reminded Emmy of a vibrant sunrise, although in this case, an explosion might be more accurate. He shifted his hands, now trembling under the table.

"I—I can go if you want, Mother."

"Leave him alone," Teddy said.

Farrah brought a hand to her face. "Leave him alone? I'm the one suffocating. How many years is he going to latch onto me? By nineteen, shouldn't he be out of my hair? You don't think of this when you adopt a small child, don't expect it. Kids are supposed to grow up and leave."

"Farrah!"

"Do I look like the maternal type to you? Honestly, I adopted him as a favor to a dead, faithful cook, and the child expects the world of me."

Emmy had heard of Matisse's humble beginnings, but she couldn't believe any mother would speak this way of her child in public.

What did Farrah expect to accomplish by this display? She had a well-deserved reputation for strategy, and this ill-advised outburst must have a purpose. To alienate Matisse? Keep him at a distance? But why?

Farrah made several additional comments causing Matisse to color, hold a hand to his mouth, and run out of the room.

The library door slammed behind him—with Gray entering almost immediately thereafter. A slim and pretty woman with short brown hair followed but remained by the door.

Gray strode over and leaned into Lew. "It's the yacht on the cove. Vivienne's arrived, and she says the boat crew is planning to leave tonight. I'm going there now."

"But the storm, son. You can't risk traveling in this weather."

"I know. The ferries have stopped, and the roads are filling up. Soon they'll be impassible—which is why I have to leave now. I'll be careful, I promise."

"Most of the guests got out after dinner," Lew said. "That was a half hour ago; good thing the rest of us are goin' anywhere tonight."

Gray shook his head. "But how safe are we here, this close to the cove? Look outside."

The three of them moved to the library window overlooking the cliff side of the house, where an angry ocean churned and thrashed. The water level had risen. Previously exposed boulders and rocks now lay underwater.

Oh, God. Had her earlier fear come true? Would the ocean flood the grounds and the house? How strong were the foundations? Were they at risk of being pulled into the inky depths of the bubbling sea?

Her instincts flared—violently—instincts she'd learned never to ignore.

Emmy turned suddenly to Gray and grabbed his sleeve. "Don't go."

"What?" He frowned and glanced down at her hand.

"I mean it, Chief Inspector. My instincts are rarely wrong, but please don't ask me to explain. I can't explain. I just know... I mean, I have a strong feeling the unimaginable is about to happen. And you should be here when it does. Not chasing the crew of a yacht, but here instead, where you're needed."

He touched her shoulder. "Nothing is going to happen."

Heat from his fingers radiated through her taffeta dress, burning her skin. She shook her head, not knowing what else to say because she knew nothing else.

165

Things were not as they seemed. It was as though each of them played their assigned part in a play—a play directed by the mysterious Stitcher.

"Slope going with you?" Lew asked.

Gray glanced towards the sergeant, who appeared to be talking self-importantly to Sita.

"No. I want to take an unofficial look inside that boat. Slope's on Vivienne's radar, remember? He could be smuggling the art himself."

"At least Slope carries a gun, son. You're dealing with shady criminals, right?"

"More than one shady criminal. Our little town seems filled with them."

A flush traveled up Emmy's face; a pebble lodged in her throat.

He spoke so calmly. Why wouldn't he listen to her?

"Something awful is going to happen," she blurted. "Something ugly and unexpected."

She wasn't usually this dramatic, and he must know it. Seymour wasn't around anywhere, or he'd back her up.

Gray rubbed a hand across his face.

By the door, his colleague, Vivienne, shuffled her feet and glared in their direction.

"You shouldn't take your eyes off the ball for a second, Chief Inspector," Emmy said. "Your wife and daughter are here, aren't they? Not for a second."

He said nothing and nodded. He even exchanged a look with his dad.

But he still left.

CHAPTER TWENTY

THE WIND JOLTED Dad's truck while it rumbled down the winding, water-logged road. Each swish of the wipers kept the windshield clear for half a second before buckets of rain obscured the view once again. Gray may as well have been driving underwater for all the visibility he had. The town lights were far away. Under the low-lying, charcoal sky, only Gray's headlights shone in the darkness.

The last time he and Slope had traveled this cliffside road down to the cove, the gray sea had glimmered in the distance, flanked by snow-capped mountain ranges on either side.

Tonight, nothing beyond twenty feet of rain-splattered asphalt remained visible—the treacherous and steep journey a reminder that man had scarcely tamed the rugged British Columbia terrain since the early pioneers logged wood for ships in the 1820s.

Gray breathed in the damp air, tinged with Vivienne's lemon and lilac scent—familiar and comforting amidst the frenzy of recent events.

What a relief to have her by his side—his colleague and friend—instead of always worrying. Vivienne's pointed features sharpened. Her hands gripped the door handle and the cushion of her seat.

"Stan and Diego plan on leaving tonight," she said. "I'm sure of it."

If the hoodlums planned to leave without their engineer, that meant they had discovered her true identity. Thank heavens she was safe. But it wasn't over yet, he reminded himself. It wasn't over yet.

"How do they plan on sailing in this weather?"

"Beats me. The guys told me to get some supplies, and when I returned, both of their rooms at the lodge were empty. Hopefully, the yacht hasn't already left."

A torrent of moving water flooded the road before them, and swerving, Gray dodged the sweeping current.

"Where did you learn about boat engines?" Gray relaxed his grip on the steering wheel. "I never knew about that back in Montreal."

"We all have a past, Chief Inspector. All of us."

Meaning that she knew better than to mention sailing in his presence—after what he had done and what he had lost.

The old wound stung, new and fresh. What the hell. Amazing how it swam below his consciousness, awaiting a weak moment to resurface.

"If the gang of smugglers are leaving, and let's presume you're right and Slope heads the gang, where did they hide the loot? You said you searched every inch of that boat."

"*Je ne sais pas.*"

"I don't know either. Priceless artifacts have to be kept dry, as well as away from prying eyes."

Vivienne stroked her chin. A single plucked eyebrow lifted. "What about this Farrah you mentioned? She owns an art gallery—a perfect hiding place."

"Which could mean she's part of the operation. An obvious choice, if Slope needed an insider."

The road flattened, and the mist separated.

Blow Hole Cove magically appeared before them—its choppy black waves jumping in violent bursts, jostling the thirty-foot yacht like a bathtub toy. A single light twinkled from the deck.

Their mission was not going to be easy.

Gray pulled into the lot and slammed the drenched brakes. The truck stopped just short of hitting a boulder.

He'd only opened the car door an inch when the wind slammed it back. Pushing harder this time, he stepped out into the onslaught. Within seconds, the surf and spray soaked his face and plastered his pants to his legs.

Vivienne was right beside him, holding a flashlight. Getting on the swaying yacht would be—

He hesitated.

But she'd already reached the boat. She held her arms up sideways to balance on the rickety plank leading to a ten-step ladder.

Gray followed closely, his heart in his throat, ready to catch her if she fell. The plank wobbled under their weight, but they quickly made it to the far end.

Water slapped his head and body while, before him, her narrow hips climbed one rail at a time. Once or twice, the wet denim back pockets of her jeans grazed his cheek, the contact sharp, abrasive.

She heaved on board, her head haloed by the single light on deck.

Gray followed, placing one foot on the swaying deck while simultaneously gripping the rail—his claw hand now dead white, his jaw clenched like a steel trap.

A yacht... in a storm.

"Let's make it quick," Vivienne yelled over the roar of the sea. Her short bangs clung to her skin. A steady stream dripped down the tip of her nose. "Who knows how strong this pile of wood is. I don't want to be on board if the mast snaps or the boat overturns. Anyone planning to go out to sea in this weather is a goddamn idiot."

Gray couldn't move.

His legs had turned into logs; he couldn't let go the rail.

The sea before him roared, as it had once before. The boat swung in all directions, like a wild, untamed dragon under his feet. Any second, he and Vivienne would fall off, and she would drown as Craig had, and he would jump in after her but not be able to see through the inky water. Not be able to feel, with his wild, useless grasps clutching at nothing.

Blood hammered through Gray's ears. He couldn't breathe—like Craig—just like Craig.

Vivienne jumped in front of him and grabbed both his arms.

"Oh God! I didn't think. You haven't... not since... and in a storm—"

He got a partial breath but not enough.

Time slowed, and so did everything else: the sea now silent, Vivienne's body stilled, the angry dragon under his feet rocking gently, as though putting a baby to sleep—before it yanked him downward.

The deck fell out from under his feet; his heart smacked against his ribs. The swaying morphed into a violent convulsion which ripped the creaking boards, shook the rails, and blurred everything.

Vivienne's voice called from afar. "I shouldn't have brought you. We're getting off—"

Three years, he hadn't stepped on a boat.

"Gray, let's go. We'll find another way."

A high-pitched shrieking echoed, "Daddy... Daddy. Help me. Help, Daddy, I'm scared."

It was followed by a thunderous crack and flash... and underwater silence. Wretched, horrific silence. All of this can't be happening. Things like this don't happen. Oh God, they don't happen.

Vivienne's shouting ripped through his haze, and he was back on the shaking yacht, before the waves. He couldn't change the past; he could never undo it.

More air entered his lungs, and it was unbearably hot. His right hand let go the rail, and the purple, snake-like scar on his wrist slithered across his skin, sharp, painful, and cutting through his flesh.

"Chief Inspector. Snap out of it!"

Vivienne's pinched face was close, swaying with the boat. A ton of lead filled his legs.

Her nails dug into his arms. "We can't stay here. Stan and Diego might be below deck. I'll take you back and come return alone."

The sound of the surf rose, and he paced his breathing. What the hell was he doing?

"I'm fine," he yelled. "We move forward."

"Non—"

"There's no time."

She shook her head. "This is my fault. I didn't think."

"Neither did I. Let's go below deck. Now."

She moved alongside him, not letting go his arm during each slippery step on the swaying deck.

The cabin appeared dark and unoccupied. As they opened the door, papers covering a table flew across the room. It took both their weights to close the door behind them.

Safely inside, she switched on the cabin light. The air felt unnaturally still; his ears rang in the relative silence.

Gray examined the floor for hidden boards. "You search that side; I'll focus here."

But the search provided no result.

"Are you sure there's no hidden compartment accessible from above deck?" he asked.

"None. I've checked every square inch of this tub."

Gray rubbed a rough hand across his stubble. It felt good to get the feeling back in his fingers. "Doesn't make sense. If they planned to smuggle artwork out of the country, they must have a hiding place."

She seemed to give it some thought. "What if this isn't the vessel they normally use. If only one piece of art needed hiding—the picture you found—why not hang it on the wall? But these walls are bare."

"And where is that piece of art now?"

He paced the plank floor, remembering something long forgotten. "This place wasn't always called Blow Hole Cove. I remember another name, abandoned thirty years ago— Smuggler's Cove?"

"Oui?"

"Our town has quite a past – the Stitcher aside."

In the late 1800's, after the Canadian Pacific Railway was built, Chinese workers who had been brought over couldn't find jobs. A man named Larry Kelly helped them cross the border, and hid them in Smugglers Cove. Later, during prohibition in the 1920's, alcohol smugglers used the cove for their purposes.

Gray recalled his last visit to the cove, with Slope. It didn't take long to retrace those steps in his mind."

"A cave." He snapped his fingers. "I noticed a narrow slit along the far rock wall, under an overhanging ridge."

"An interim hiding place for stolen art?"

"Until someone retrieves it, and they take it out to sea. But consider what we know: the crew plans to leave today—without you—and yet, the yacht's still here. The culprits are waiting for someone."

"Someone who's supposed to board before the three of them leave? That's suicide."

Gray recalled the most recent weather forecast and shook his head. "The storm's hit earlier than expected. Initially, all reports said the brunt of it would miss our coast. Whoever made this plan didn't foresee the change in conditions. They took a risk—"

"And now they're stranded," Vivienne said. "But who is it?"

Gray felt the walls of the small cabin moving in. He had to get out of.

"When I know that, I'll be able to identify the Stitcher."

"What?" Vivienne shook her head. "You're sure the two crimes are connected?"

He recalled again the art critic's car found a few miles from Emmy's farm. The old photograph he'd shown Dad.

"We have to get to that cave," he said. "Now."

Once on deck, Gray switched on the flashlight. They retraced their steps, backed down the ladder, and crossed the wobbly plank.

Waves crashed the pebbled beach, and Gray ran to the edge of the nearby cliff where he'd seen the cave entrance.

Darkness made it harder to find, and he felt along the protruding rock edge while Vivienne flashed the torch.

Sharp cuts of sandstone and shale lined the face of the cliff, the granitic surface a product of thousands of years of enduring sea and wind, and collisions between the mountains and the hot ocean plate.

"There!" Gray pointed to a break in the rock.

The ten-foot-tall crack in the side of the cliff was wide enough to accommodate an average-sized man. He squeezed through before Vivienne followed, trying to ignore that pungent scent of bat-droppings. Hoping a shoal of bats didn't fly into him.

Five feet in, the crevice ballooned open into a cavern with sweat-beaded stone walls; wafts of fresh sea air made it inside in bursts.

The sand rolled under Gray's feet. An eerie howling traveled from the cave's mouth towards the darkened abyss ahead. Vivienne breathed fast and hard behind him, her mouth almost at his ear, and the gentle swell of her breasts at times brushing his back.

"I want to get the hell out of here," she said, her whisper loud in the closed space.

"Me too. Look along the walls. They must have hidden something in here, or else why park the yacht nearby? Why plan an escape from Blowhole Cove?"

Now, her breath brushed his neck, making his hairs stand erect.

A shuffle from the left made him turn. Before he could swing the flashlight, two shadowed figures pounced out of the darkness; one hit Gray over the head.

Pain shot through his skull and light sparked behind his eyes. No time to stop, even as his knees buckled, and things went black—only for a moment before reality returned.

He lifted the torch. Mossy, bleeding walls showed in the oblong light, and he ran.

Vivienne struggled to her feet a second after him, her panting coming close behind him.

Outside the cavern opening, the cold air hit him like a shovel, and water bursts out of the blow hole straight ahead.

Two ghostly silhouettes shot across the beach and onto the paved lot before turning a sharp corner towards the road. One of the men carried something in his hands.

Gray went after them, hearing Vivienne's shouts but not able to make out the words.

The wind direction shifted and pushed him from behind, easing the pain in his head and the burn in his thighs.

Wetness slid down his cheek. All that mattered was catching them and finding what they carried.

He turned the corner and nearly slipped on the rain-slick asphalt. Portions of the road lay pooled and flooded, making each step treacherous. Twice, his ankle turned in a pothole camouflaged by the muddy water; with a little luck, the heftier and slower of the two men who carried the parcel would suffer a similar fate.

From Gray's thoughts to the other man's feet, it happened: the man missed his footing and dived into a pothole, teetered for a second before falling flat on his face with a splash.

The crook had the good sense to throw the object clear—a large, rectangular package wrapped in brown paper and tied with string—towards his partner, two strides ahead, but the other man didn't see.

He instead turned towards a dilapidated truck by the side of the road, giving Gray a first clear glimpse of his face.

It was Stan, the captain, from Vivienne's boat, who resembled a wide-jawed Neanderthal with supraorbital ridges and eyebrows you could camp under.

He glared at Gray before noticing the fallen package midway between them on the road. Gray raced towards it, seeing Stan do the same.

Three meters from the object, Gray leaped forward and stretched one arm out towards the parcel—just as Stan's weight crashed into him. And two fists made contact with Gray's face.

He felt his tooth cut the inside of his mouth, let go the package, and flipped Stan onto his back before returning the favor with a solid punch of his own. The fake sea captain lay dazed in a muddy puddle.

"Don't move," Vivienne yelled, aiming a gun at Stan. She stood drenched, feet wide apart, trying to keep her balance in the circling gusts of wind.

Gray spit out salty blood, wiped his mouth with his hand. His head felt crushed inside a vice. To his right, the other man from the yacht lay unconscious in the puddle, face down.

"Chief, Diego—"

Gray pushed up, stumbled to where Diego lay and turned him over. Hopefully, he hadn't already drowned.

The man wasn't breathing.

"Keep Stan covered," he told Vivienne. "I'm going to try and resuscitate his accomplice."

But there was no need. The sprawled man spluttered and coughed almost immediately. Diego opened his eyes. His head fell back when he saw Vivienne with the gun.

"Good," Gray said, stumbling towards the rapidly soaking parcel.

After grabbing the large package, he shot towards Stan's truck, got into the cab, cut the string with his teeth, and removed the wrapping.

"What's in it?" Vivienne shouted, still covering the two men.

The paper clung to the surface, but water hadn't yet penetrated the canvas.

"A painting," he replied.

He examined the abstract scene—familiar, and at the heart of this case.

As Gray expected, it was the same painting as in the faded black and white snapshot found in the victim's Vancouver apartment.

The Stitcher's victim, Donovan Price, must have been searching for this piece of art. But why? And who had prevented him from finding it?

CHAPTER TWENTY-ONE

EMMY PLACED HER HAND on the library window and felt the cold glass numb her fingertips. She lifted them; the resulting imprints faded before her eyes. Further away, foaming waves crashed against the cliff side and jetted into their small cove.

She'd left the others in the salon, needing some space from Seymour's kind attention and also unable to keep her eyes off this view and the alarming rise of the water level.

What did it feel like to drown? To be swept away by a watery vastness? She suddenly knew herself to be small, minuscule. And being alone in this room only cemented that impression. She should be with the others.

Right now, Seymour was occupied elsewhere in the mansion. Gray had assigned him the task of watching Sita, Noelle, and Lew. How he could manage to be in three places at once, Emmy didn't know, but Seymour was more than capable of handling a challenge.

She moved towards the door, when an ear-piercing howl echoed from the corridor.

Footsteps ran in her direction.

Emmy shot out of the room, flew down the paneled hall leading to the back terrace of the house.

When she turned the corner, a solid chest slammed into her and threw her to the wall. Pain shot through her shoulder.

Matisse also fell on his behind.

"What is it?" She moved over him. "Did you scream?"

His bloodless lips opened and closed. No words formed.

"Tell me. What happened?"

His rigid arm rose as if of its own volition, and a trembling finger pointed towards the end of the hall which led to the back French doors.

"Mom—" he said. His breath smelled of alcohol.

"Farrah? Something's happened to Farrah?"

"Me and... and Teddy. On the terrace."

Emmy shook his shoulders. Had her fears come true, and did another of the Stitcher's victim's lie mutilated nearby? No matter what her disagreements with Matisse's mother, she'd never wish this upon anyone.

"Oh, God. What's happened? Tell me!"

But he began heaving and sobbing and wouldn't stop. Shutting her eyes, Emmy tried to make the image go away. Of Farrah strangled and sutured. No, no. Not another death.

Her feet moved of their own volition down the corridor. The pungent metallic odor of blood—imagined or real—assailed her nostrils. Her body worked on automatic, disconnected from her head, and in some distant horrific recess of her mind, saw herself lying helpless and hurt.

The French doors to the terrace lay closed ahead. She pushed them open and stood on the wet patio, rain slamming down like shards of glass, the wind swirling all around and fluttering the taffeta frills of her ridiculous dress.

Darkness enveloped her like a black hole.

"Farrah!"

The raging storm ate Emmy's words.

She should have gotten more details from Matisse. Would he still be down the corridor?

A porch light flickered on and off—long enough to see that this interlocked stone terrace stood empty.

Voices from behind came closer, bringing two men suddenly upon her.

Teddy's low voice boomed out. "The light's not working. You got the torch, Slope?"

Something blinded Emmy's eyes. "Move that away from me," she said.

Slope lowered the beam onto the ground. "What the hell are you doing out here? This is a crime scene. You need to go back into the house."

"I'm also a doctor. If Farrah's injured, maybe I can help."

Emmy could also have told him the terrace was empty. She wanted to ask him to look further out, beyond the bushes, but nothing else came out. The last few minutes in the gale had parched her throat; every inch of her was becoming more drenched and numb by the second.

Teddy moved in close. She couldn't see his face, only an outline of his head, with the flashlight beam darting across the terrace in the background as Slope searched the area.

"Emmy. I left Matisse to watch Farrah. Where's the boy gone?"

"Where's Inspector Gray?"

"I don't know. He isn't back."

She bit her lip, tasting salt. Her teeth chattered, and her knees banged against one another.

What had Teddy said? Watch Farrah? Was she alive or dead?

Emmy's wet hair blew across her face, and he shifted it from her eyes. The shaking made it hard to stand. He led her inside into the dimly-lit hall, but they stood before the open doors to be able to hear Slope's call.

Teddy glared at her, the lines around his mouth appearing twice as deep as they had an hour earlier.

"She's dead," he said.

"Farrah?"

"Delilah. The minute I saw Farrah lyin' there, I knew Gray was right. That was my little girl on the beach he found. I don't know what I thought – that it must be a mistake – that she'd only gone away like she sometimes did. But she ain't coming home. Ever." He hunched over. "My poor baby."

Seconds mattered. Emmy had to help him focus. "Farrah's not here."

"What you say? Where's that boy? I told him to watch the body."

The body?

"You mean, she's dead?"

"I gotta go find Matisse," Teddy said. "Or maybe I should stay with Slope, help him search. This kinda wind don't move bodies off a terrace."

So Farrah had been lying on the terrace, as Matisse said. Emmy hesitated. She swallowed twice before asking the question burning a hole in her mind. "Was she—"

Teddy nodded. "Her lips were stitched, and she looked god-awful. Same as—" He swallowed his words.

Same as his daughter, Delilah. Except he couldn't say it out loud. And yet, his voice now sounded calm, too calm.

"I'll go find Matisse." She led him by the arm back to the terrace. "I'll take care of the boy, don't worry. You help Slope. Even if he finds Farrah's body, I don't trust him. We need to preserve all evidence of the crime until Chief Inspector Gray returns."

He stumbled like an old man toward Slope's smudged and bobbing flashlight in the distance.

A hot draft greeted her in the hall, the clinging dress now feeling like a clammy plant against her skin, oozing secretions.

Emmy longed to rip it off, and some part of her dared to traipse around in her underwear if only to be dry again, but she didn't. When was the last time she felt this trapped within herself?

Pushing forward on stiff joints, she turned the corner and found Matisse where she'd left him, eyes glaring, as though staring at a fate worse than death. He sat in a puddle which briefly morphed into blood red before turning translucent once again.

She was losing it.

"Tell me what happened." Emmy shook him hard. "What did you see?"

His red tongue protruded out of a gaping mouth, reminding her of an open wound—but he only mouthed the words.

Emmy shook him again; his head rolled on his neck.

"Let's get you a drink." She helped him up and into the adjacent room—an office—and plopped the boy's dead weight onto an upholstered chair.

After pouring out whatever amber liquid sat in a crystal decanter, she brought the drink to his mouth, forced him to take two large gulps before taking away the glass.

Urgency, raw and powerful, surged through her. All those years of medical training. If Farrah was still alive, they had to find her. Save her.

It could be hours before Gray returned—if tonight at all. Without Lew or Seymour nearby, everything fell on Emmy's shoulders. And she wasn't about to go traipsing around the mansion looking for them. She was the doctor on the scene; Slope couldn't be trusted.

Matisse's voice squeaked, "I... I—"

"What happened?"

"Teddy and me, w-we took a stroll after having a drink. We came down the hall." Matisse reached for the glass and gulped it down. "There was a flash from outside the French doors, and we ran to investigate." He starting sobbing again.

"You opened the doors." Impatience ground at her insides. "What did you see?"

"Mother," he mouthed, silently before letting out another ear-melting shriek.

Emmy slammed her hand over his mouth. "No, I want answers, now."

The boy kept shaking his head. How could she make him understand the urgency?

"I have a bad feeling about this, Matisse. We're all in terrible danger. A killer is on the loose, do you understand? And there's no one around to protect us. We have to be sharp."

He nodded. "She... she lay there—strangled."

"Her lips sutured?"

"Sewn together like a doll, all pale, bloodless, no life. I jumped to pick her up, but Teddy held me back."

"After you screamed?"

"Yes, but he said one of us had to go get help while the other stayed with the body."

And Teddy had chosen the victim's son to stay, instead of being at his wife's side while the boy went for help.

But that was unfair. He would have judged Matisse to be unreliable in the circumstances—like a frightened toddler facing the lifeless body of his beloved mother. And Matisse had loved her—perhaps a little too much, and in a way Emmy did not wish to understand.

"What happened then?" she said.

"I saw her lying there, her hair whipping in the wind, rain scarring her beautiful face, so helpless and hurt."

"And you ran and slammed into me in the hall. She's no longer there, Matisse. Your mother's body is gone."

"What?"

Blood drained from his face; his eyes bugged out. No one could have faked that reaction, Emmy was sure of it. Matisse was frightened and confused.

"Farrah isn't on the terrace," she repeated. "Slope and Teddy are out there searching for her. You know what that means? Someone removed the body after you left, just like in the other two murders."

"Other two?"

How could he not know? He must be in shock.

"The art critic from Vancouver that I found strangled at my facility? And Delilah—who Chief Inspector James discovered on the beach by his cottage."

His jaw clenched.

"Tell me what you know," Emmy blurted.

"I know nothing. Who could have taken Mother?"

"The killer, of course. The same way he took the others. Any one of us could be next."

The office window blew open and threw rain and debris into the room.

Emmy jumped up and pushed it closed. She turned the latch. "We're trapped in this house. The roads are impassable, Chief Inspector James isn't here, and we have to protect ourselves. Three dead bodies in as many days are too much, even for me. Do you hear me? Even for me."

She stood and held out a hand.

He accepted her help and rose—an unlikely ally in the dubious group. She couldn't ignore his being first on the scene;

the person who found the body automatically rose in the line of prime suspects, or so she'd heard.

The main thing right now was to join the others and not be alone with any one person. By now, Teddy or Slope must have herded all the others into either the salon or the library. The salon seemed the likelier place.

She opened the office door and looked left and right. Empty.

Half carrying Matisse, she rushed down the hall with ears tuned to every noise, save the monstrous cacophony outside. He smelled of sweat and alcohol, both unpleasant.

As they passed a window overlooking the back yard, Slope's darting flashlight could be seen out in the open grounds. She kept going.

There had been three deaths that she knew of—four if you included the first Stitcher killing. Who knew how many more Slope had pushed under the rug? Sorting out allies from possible enemies proved easy: Lew and Seymour could be trusted, she was sure of it. The others couldn't. But Seymour might have left with Gray, and Lew couldn't fight a crazed killer. If it came down to it, Emmy would have to use brute force herself.

She needed a weapon.

A knife—no, a gun? Where the hell could she find one?

"Does Teddy keep a revolver?" she asked Matisse.

"Yeah, but he'll never give it to you."

They reached the salon. Four sets of eyes shot in her direction. She practically shoved Matisse down onto a chintz armchair, but he wouldn't stay. Within seconds, he had bolted out of the room.

"Has Teddy told you?" she asked the group.

185

Sita paced the room while her toddler slept on the sofa. Lew sat clutching his cane in a white-fisted grip, while a few other guests paced the room. Seymour was absent.

"No," Sita said in a tone which implicitly blamed Emmy for any evils which might have occurred.

Water trickled into Emmy's eyes; she ground out her words. "Has anyone seen a stranger in the house tonight?"

"Why are you asking that?" the other woman said.

"Just answer the question."

"Reggie's in charge here, not you. And when Gray returns, he'll probably take over." Sita said.

Emmy leaned in close to Lew, "You saw no one? And where's Butch? I expected to find him with Teddy."

"I haven't seen him since we arrived. I thought he went to the farm earlier today."

"He did. Teddy sent him to get some overnight things from my cabin and secure the rest of the forensic sites. That was before the storm worsened. Maybe he didn't make it back?"

The older man's hand shook. "Has there been another murder? Teddy didn't say much. He took Slope aside, and the self-congratulatory fool gave us all orders to stay in this room come hell or high water. Which I have to anyway, let's face it. I'm not running away from a killer in a hurry."

He hadn't asked the identity of the victim. But Lew James was no one's fool. Only one party, other than Seymour, was noticeably absent.

She'd been the most vocal person all night, and perhaps each of them felt a tinge of guilt for not wishing her back, for not missing the sharps and flats of her demanding voice.

Lew may as well know the truth. "Teddy and Matisse found Farrah dead on the back terrace. Matisse didn't stay with her, and the body disappeared, like the others. We desperately need your son."

The old man frowned, his face as cracked as the bare ground by Emmy's cabin during a dry spell.

A sheen of sweat coated his upper lip, lending his body the stale smell of aging flesh. She wanted to reach out and hold him, for fear he might disintegrate in a puff of dust at any moment.

"Seymour wouldn't stay in the room," Lew said. "Too much blood in the water for him to manage patience. Just as well, you need someone to protect you. And he isn't the killer, Emmy. I guarantee you. Do as I say and stick with John Seymour."

If I can find him, she thought, decidedly unwilling to traverse the wide paneled corridors alone.

But the prospect of Seymour shadowing her every step didn't thrill her either. Both alternatives made her wish Gray would return, and soon. With or without that pretty French detective of his.

"I'm going to go look for John," Emmy said.

"No."

Emmy wouldn't reveal her real reason for leaving the group—to search for a weapon. She had a feeling that before night's end, she would need it.

If a needle-wielding killer came anywhere near her, she wanted a revolver in her grip. Not a knife. Not a club.

The question remained, where would Teddy keep his? And had he already retrieved it?

Lew placed a hand on her shoulder. "I'd go out there with you... but—" He glanced towards Noelle.

"I know. Don't take your eyes off your granddaughter. And keep that cane handy."

He pointed toward the fireplace. Emmy nodded.

Poker in hand, she left the salon, firmly closing the doors behind her.

Every bit of her concentration went toward listening and feeling her way through the empty halls.

Matisse was again somewhere out there, lurking; so were Seymour and a stranger—outside the mansion or within?

For the first time, Emmy considered a disturbing possibility: that the Stitcher was one of them. If someone attacked her, she planned to squash them like a bug and use their body for forensic research afterward.

Poker held up high, Emmy crept back to the office she and Matisse had earlier left.

After closing the door, conscious of the hinges creaking and the slight clicking of the lock, she scanned the room to make sure it was empty. No one hid behind the window curtains; no one could come up from behind.

The desk drawers yielded nothing. A cabinet in one corner lay crammed with papers, mementos best thrown out.

A letter opener on the desk might work. And yet, the thought of going back out into the hall, unarmed, frightened her.

Emmy forced herself to concentrate.

All three victims had been strangled. The Stitcher attacked from behind—in which case, a sharp object, thrust backward between the ribs, would be more effective than a gun anyway.

She gripped the letter opener like a dagger, and peeked out the door.

No one.

A loud thud echoed down the hall, coming from the foyer. Followed by a slam. The door?

Relief flooded through her. Emmy ran towards sounding footsteps.

Gray James was back. Thank God, he was back.

CHAPTER TWENTY-TWO

THE TRUCK'S GALLOPING high beams illuminated the slick roads, but they couldn't penetrate the storm's wall of slashing rain and debris beyond twenty feet.

Gray's insides felt eaten. An inner voice screamed at him for leaving Noelle, Dad, and the others unprotected when Emmy had begged him to stay.

Had he made another fatal mistake? The stench of fear stuck to his nostrils, drifting upward from every pore of his clammy body.

He had to get back as fast as he could. He had to get back in one piece.

Vivienne's eyes met his and softened. She could always read him like a book. She turned towards the two handcuffed men in the back seat, looking happy with her catch, triumphant even.

"Is Inspector Slope the head of your operation?" she said. They hit a bump, and she gripped the back of her seat.

Gray glanced into the rear-view mirror.

The wide-jawed Neanderthal, Stan, pressed his lips together in a line. In the truck's interior, his gray-pink skin resembled that of a mouse. The other man, Diego, stared out the window long-faced.

"Slope couldn't tell a Monet from a Rembrandt," Gray said to Vivienne. He would sooner bill Slope as the Stitcher than a smuggler.

"There could be another accomplice."

The sergeant craved prestige, wealth, power—not a life forever on the run. He might kill to gain Delilah's fortune, and yet by all accounts they weren't married. Or perhaps, Teddy would kill to keep his estate from Slope's hands. The same applied to Farrah.

A shard of lightning—suspended and white as opaque glass—lit the road and valley ahead.

It left a redness on his retina before his vision cleared. Thunder rang through his ears.

At any moment, they might catapult off the cliff's edge and fly through the water-logged sky—ending Gray's pain, and the uncertainty of what might happen next.

The wipers hummed a monotonous tune.

He forced himself to focus on the case. Art held the central spot in the mystery—figures and facts circling it like planets around a blazing sun. People could kill for a twenty, never mind a priceless painting—but he risked forging an imaginary link where none existed. Coincidences occurred all the time.

"Dad might be able to tell us more when he looks at this painting," Gray said. "The photograph was old and worn."

Maybe, maybe not.

A film of sweat formed within the stubble above his lip. His tongue tasted like a rotting cut of meat in his mouth.

Just then, an unexpected left turn made him twist the steering.

He wrestled with the screeching wheels until the vehicle stopped its sideways motion. Gray breathed heavy before shifting back into gear and moving on.

"What the hell, man!" Stan looked ashen in the rear-view mirror. "You trying to kill us or something?"

"Tryin' to scare us, more likely," the other crook said.

Vivienne slammed the seat. "Shut up, you two."

Only a mile further to go.

"No one's leaving the mansion tonight," he said. "Not in this weather. I'll get Teddy to give you a room next to Noelle's."

She understood him perfectly. "Oui."

They reached Pine Cove Mansion a few minutes later.

The truck shrieked to a halt. Gray jumped out and motioned the two prisoners to lead the climb up the mansion steps. Vivienne clutched the painting to her chest and wrapped it inside her coat.

Once inside, drenched coat off, Gray covered the two thugs. He hated the feel of a gun in his hands, and his gripping the trigger with his right claw hand didn't go unnoticed by her or the others. Gray could not have fired it if he had wanted to. She took the weapon and motioned the two prisoners down the hall.

"Take these two to the library. I don't want them near the others." Meaning he didn't want them anywhere near his daughter. "I'll send Slope to help you."

Emmy flew down the hall to greet him, looking entirely different from when he'd left.

Her dress and hair were soaked. Mascara ran down her cheeks, giving her a raccoon appearance she hadn't bothered to wipe away—and she held a letter opener in her hand like a dagger.

What the hell had happened in his absence? "Noelle! Is she okay?" he shouted.

"What? What does that have to do with—"

"My daughter! Has the Stitcher struck again?" How dense was she to not understand his panic at seeing her wielding a weapon? He wouldn't yell at her again, but it took all his control to shove the rage down. He had to talk to someone human, like Dad or Seymour.

He ground out the words. "Where is everyone?"

"In the salon." Her voice trailed behind him. "Don't you want to know what's happened? Where have you been?"

He burst across the foyer and into the salon, the atmosphere within entirely different from when he'd left. Tension hung heavy in the air, and Lew and another couple turned as he entered.

But it was Sita who ran over and clasped both arms around him, trembling. Noelle lay asleep on the sofa. Thank God.

"Where have you been? You can't fly out of here without telling me. I was worried sick, and you know there's been another killing."

Gray moved to Noelle, lifted a strand of hair from her delicate and perfect forehead. "Who?"

"Farrah."

Gray swung around. "You're kidding."

"Afraid not." Seymour stood at the door, heaving and out of breath. "I need you to come with me, James. Now."

Seymour had obviously failed at disarming Emmy, who still held the letter opener in her grip.

"In a minute." Gray took the painting to Lew. "Dad—"

"I'll watch them both, and take a look at the painting. You go with Seymour."

Gusts of wind blew at them as they walked the hall. Someone must have left the back French doors to the terrace open.

Seymour reached the open French doors first, followed by Gray and Emmy.

He turned to her. "Tell me what happened."

Emmy's succinct explanation—about finding Matisse, the subsequent disappearance of the body—went a long way to changing Gray's opinion of her. He could use someone this logical and tough on the team, but Seymour was shaking his head and pulling Gray by the arm.

"I went looking for Emmy after Slope herded us into the salon." He spoke as they ran to the west side of the house. "And I found Farrah's body."

"You found it?" Emmy said. "Where?"

Seymour didn't answer. What awaited them on the next turn stopped Gray in his tracks.

Emmy gasped beside him. She must be reliving their recent mutual experience of finding the Stitcher's victims. She must be experiencing what he now felt: acid burning his insides; a fury strong enough to smash through the hall walls.

Farrah lay on her back, not spread-eagled in a degrading posture—but positioned carefully, as though peacefully asleep.

Her hands were folded across her abdomen, the overly-large engagement ring twinkling obscenely under the overhead bulb.

Her blond strands lay in a gentle curve above her head. But she'd still been mutilated.

Gray couldn't believe what lay beside the body and turned to Seymour. "The suture needle and retractor were left again—"

Emmy's head shot up. "Again?"

Gray clammed up. She knew first-hand that no sutures or medical instruments were found beside the victim at the body farm. And he'd reported nothing of finding such items near Delilah's body.

Emmy slowly rose. "The only time the Stitcher left his implements behind was fifteen years ago—Mrs. Franklin mentioned it to me."

Gray faced Seymour. "When did you find her?"

"A minute ago. I heard you in the hall and got you right away. Nothing's changed—this is how I found her." He looked up. "The Stitcher's here, in the house. He could even be one of us."

"What do you estimate as the time of death?"

"Recent. Very recent." Seymour ran a hand through his hair. "Maybe thirty minutes. Look at the older bruises on the neck, along with the new strangulation marks."

Gray had already seen them. "At least we can exclude Vivienne's two sailors from the suspect list. Slope, Teddy, the remaining guests—even Matisse could have done it."

With no hope of getting SOCO here tonight, Seymour was taking pictures from every angle with his phone.

Emmy kneeled before the body, her face intense, her red lips slightly open. Here was an excellent witness—one which Gray couldn't afford to ignore.

She said something unexpected. "One point four centimeters."

Gray leaned in. "What did you say?"

"This suturing is coarse, amateurish compared to that of the victim I found at the body farm." She looked up. "It isn't neat, and the spacing between stitches is over two-and-a-half centimeters. The man at the body farm had his lips sutured with each stitch one point four centimeters in length."

"You noticed that?"

"Of course I noticed it."

Seymour chimed in. "Something else is different—this red and black stuff over her mouth and cheeks. She wore pale pink lipstick tonight, I'm sure of it. Why would the Stitcher apply makeup to his victim?" He shook his head. "I don't understand the change in modus operandi." He slapped his head. "God, James, do we have two copycats now?"

"Not in the way you think."

Gray stood. "We can't leave her here—not with others roaming the mansion. Take a look around, Doctor. See what else you can find in the vicinity, and after that, get back to the salon as soon as possible. The situation is perilous. We have more than one killer with us tonight."

Seymour and Emmy stared, unblinking.

With one or two more facts garnered with Dad's help, Gray hoped to pinpoint the killer, tonight.

"I'll lock the body in one of the upstairs bedrooms," he said. "Where are Slope and Teddy, not to mention Butch?"

Emmy had gone dead white. Her silk hair stuck to her neck and shoulders.

"Butch went to my cottage," she said. "I don't know if he made it back. I haven't seen the other two, but last I noticed, they were searching the grounds outside for Farrah's body."

"In the storm?" Gray couldn't believe it. "With women and children left alone in the house?"

"In all fairness, Slope told me to stay in the salon." Seymour looked contrite. "I had to go out and find Emmy, though. That's when the shit hit the fan."

Gray lifted Farrah's bony, lifeless form easily, cradling the head with his shoulder. No matter how she had treated others, Farrah didn't deserve this.

"Don't go near Butch, either of you. Do you understand?"

"Butch?" Emmy said. "I don't believe it. He's too thick to orchestrate these complicated murders. If you suspect him, that means… that means Teddy is the brains behind this. He's the killer, isn't he?"

"The other bodies—" Gray stopped mid-step. "They're here, in the mansion. Butch brought them back. Don't go near him, either of you, and don't let him into the salon. Lock the door from the inside when you get there. I have to check in with Dad and then Vivienne."

Seymour had reached his side. "There's nothing more I can do here. I'll go with you."

"No."

"What about Slope and Teddy. They can help."

"I can't trust either of them. Not before I tie up the last few details."

"You're juggling too many balls, and you know it," Seymour said. "They're all going to come crashing down."

Gray carried Farrah upstairs, pausing half-way. "I can live with that, so long as nothing happens to my family. Do you understand? I need you, John."

Seymour nodded, his face dark, his shoulders tight. He lingered a second longer.

After they entered the salon, Gray moved up to the first bedroom. He placed Farrah on the bed and pulled the door shut.

While he made his way back downstairs, a crash sounded from below, followed by a shot.

Vivienne.

The sound of thudding feet made him fly downstairs. A blur of wet coats and dark hair passed passed below; a gust of howling wind spun upward; the front door slammed shut.

Stumbling, Vivienne tried to follow, but a cut on her forehead bled profusely.

Goddammit, he'd left her too long. Too many balls in the air, Seymour had said.

"How badly are you hurt?"

Taking her by the waist, he half-carried her to the others and banged on the door. "It's Gray. Open up."

Vivienne caught her breath. "I'm okay. One of them smashed a lamp, and when I looked, the other swung his handcuffed fists at my face. I feel okay. Don't worry."

"A couple of minutes and I would have been with you. They won't go far in this storm." The salon door opened.

"Where can they hide?" Vivienne said.

"The guest house out back, or else the cellars, if they can re-enter the house undetected."

Seymour didn't bother with questions, reading Vivienne's injury and the lack of two thugs accurately.

Together, they helped her onto a settee, and without anyone noticing Vivienne's gun was moved to Seymour's jacket pocket.

Gray turned to find Teddy and Slope coming in, but he had no time for questions. He faced Slope.

"Where have you been? We arrested the two seamen by the cove. They're art smugglers."

"Are they?" The sergeant's inscrutable expression gave nothing away.

"They attacked Vivienne, and now they've escaped. Stay here and protect the others, in case they return." Gray took Teddy aside. "I need you with me. Do you have all the keys to the grounds?"

Teddy looked around and shrugged. "I got 'em in my pocket. What're we lookin' for? And where's Matisse?" His eyes widened. "You don't think—"

"That the Stitcher will strike again? Possibly."

"You know who it is?"

"Yes—and where the killer left your daughter's body. I have to retrieve it as evidence."

He expected Teddy to demand more answers before handing over the keys, but he didn't. Could Gray be wrong? Had he made the most catastrophic of mistakes confiding in Teddy?

He moved towards Dad next.

Lew stood up, gripped the painting in one hand and the cane in the other. He wasn't about to let either go.

"What do you think?" Gray made certain no one could hear them.

"A genuine Picasso. I'd bet my life on it." His legs wobbled, and he sat back down. "Son, I can't tell you how nervous I am about having this thing with us. It's priceless, and many a thief would go through us all to get it."

"I know. We have to make it through the night. By the morning, the weather will let up, and we can get out of here."

"You're staying here." Lew didn't state it as a question.

"I can't, Dad. We need those two first bodies as evidence to convict the killer."

"That isn't your problem—it's Slope's."

Gray met Lew's eyes, leaving the rest unspoken. They both knew what needed doing. The Stitcher had to be caught and put to rest. For everyone's sake.

Lew hugged him and turned away. "Go, but make damn sure you come back. I can't lose another boy." His voice trailed away. "I won't survive it."

CHAPTER TWENTY-THREE

WHEN HE WAS in the hall alone, Gray stopped and listened—for any sounds other than the thrashing storm outside and voices drifting from the salon.

A few days ago, Teddy had mentioned that Butch kept furniture and other items stored in the cellar and nearby shed. It seemed the best place to temporarily conceal bodies never meant to be found—amidst the discarded residue of a hundred years.

If Butch had already buried the victims somewhere in the thousands of miles of BC wilderness, he would have had to travel long and far, and they were lost forever. Gray didn't think the property manager had yet had time for proper disposal, and kept his fingers crossed.

The steps leading to the basement stood in a side corridor off the foyer.

Inside the damp cellar, Gray moved around blindly before finding the switch. The three consecutive low-ceilinged rooms only revealed dusty portraits, trunks, and generations of detritus encased in spider webs.

If Butch kept the evidence on the property, it wasn't here, where all the household might look.

That left the guest house and attached shed.

Gray ran back upstairs, swung open the French doors leading to the back terrace and lawn, keys and torch in hand.

The wind and rain smashed his skin. To his left, waves crashed in the cove, pounding against the rocks, the water level alarmingly high. Much of the lawn lay flooded by the sea.

He stomped across the ankle-deep water for about fifty meters before reaching the guest house and shed.

Directly behind, pines creaked and swayed, their thick branches threatening to snap and plummet thirty feet to the ground.

The first key in Teddy's chain didn't fit the shed lock. It took three tries before one did—but the eight by ten-foot structure contained little more than a lawn mower and other tools and implements. There were no bodies. No clues to where they might be.

He covered the few steps down to the sunken guest house entrance where Farrah had her painting studio. He found the right key and turned the lock.

Inside, the familiar scent of paint and turpentine assailed his nostrils. Was it only two days ago that he climbed these steps with Teddy?

But this time, the view out the windows didn't reveal the beautiful Pacific and trees: instead, rain slashed the glass, giving Farrah's studio an underwater feel.

Every instinct made him want to bolt out of there, but he disciplined himself to stay. If this cabin had a cellar as well—that might be what Teddy had referred to when he said only Butch went into the cellar—beneath the guest house, not Pine Cove mansion.

He stepped into the sunken foyer to look. Only one very solid, oak door—with a sliding bolt on the surface—could have led to the cellar.

It took eight tries on the keychain before hitting gold.

The circular staircase leading downward was pitch black, dank, and rotten. Loud squeaking preceded a flash of movement at his feet. Gray swung the torch.

Rats sprang at him and flew upstairs to the house. He clenched his fist and took in a few steadying breaths. Fleeing rodents could mean only one terrible thing.

It wasn't too late to turn back. Dad was right; he should leave it to Slope. Except, without this evidence, nothing would be right again. The bodies had to be down here.

Gray's breathing came quick and heavy. Each step into the damp darkness brought a real fear he was brave enough to acknowledge. The sooner he searched the cellar, the sooner he could get out.

Halfway down, he heard the expected roar.

On the bottom step, water gushed into his already drenched shoes, sprang forward, now reaching his ankles.

Sharp debris hit his leg—the edge of a wooden crate?—and the bobbing of his torchlight revealed water-logged tools, clothes, even a kite.

What the hell was he doing? He turned back—until Gray saw a mannequin's hand, with painted nails, swimming towards him as though riding a rapid.

Except, it wasn't a mannequin; it was a woman. He recognized the coat from the beach and Delilah's mutilated face which now appeared more grotesque and bloated.

He could stay long enough to grab her body safely.

She jetted towards him like a ghostly apparition, and he steeled himself not to jump back. With the torch in his claw grip, he grabbed her with his left hand.

It slammed against him, and he fell face down in the water— just as something else hard hit his head.

202

Coughing and sputtering, Gray came up to get a lungful of musty air. Delilah had hit the bottom of the stairs and was being shoved and beaten by other debris.

He pushed himself up on stiff legs. The frigid, salty water now reached his thighs.

Somewhere, past the inky depths of the cellar, lay uncharted caves leaving into the eyes of the cove—similar caves and caverns to the one he'd discovered by the yacht miles away at Smuggler's Cove.

Pine Mansion had a similar smuggling history. Caves, which were generally above ground, were flooding in the storm. In minutes this cellar would be under water.

He lifted Delilah's stiff body, and his arms ached. Wet clothes and fatigue weighed him down.

Each step up the winding staircase felt impossible. The current grew stronger by the second and pulled at Gray's legs until its teeth finally let go when he touched the first dry step. There was still a long way up before he reached the lit foyer.

Another eight or nine steps and he'd be there. He couldn't think about reaching the top or carrying Delilah across the now more flooded lawn. Anyone could be out there waiting for him, and Gray no longer had the strength for a fight.

One step at a time.

He made it to the top. Delilah fell out of his arms and rolled onto the entrance tile.

Heaving a sigh of relief, Gray closed his eyes — when a figure rushed forward—eyes bright and mad, face possessed in a frenzy—and slammed the door in his face.

Gray stumbled back, the torch still in one hand, the other grasping for the rail—Matisse's crazed face burned into memory forever.

The fall ended when he smashed into the curved wall. Ice-cold seawater pounded his left hip.

In seconds, the staircase and sunken entrance would flood to the water level of the lawns outside. Gray took deep breaths. Icy hands encircled his chest.

Struggling to his feet, he flew to the cellar door and tried the handle. The door wouldn't budge. He slammed the rock-solid oak with his shoulder, but Matisse must have engaged the bolt. No light shone from underneath. No one answered Gray's calls.

The water's push might break the door on its hinges, or it might not. Either way, Gray would drown before that happened. He needed another plan—quick—before the air ran out.

How far before the cellar met the caverns of the cove? Might the distance be forty or fifty feet?

Once the stairwell filled—provided the door held—water would stop pouring in, and Gray could swim. He was a damn strong swimmer, even in this state. But it was a long shot.

Without the torch, he was dead already. He shifted it to his good hand.

Water climbed his neck, lifting him to the ceiling. Every inch of his skin felt jabbing needles, and he risked hypothermia before making it to the cove.

Five more seconds… four… three. It inched up Gray's face. He arched his neck for the last breath before all air disappeared—preparing: flexing and positioning his muscles and opening his eyes to the salty and frigid sting.

The bright torch beam shot forward, bouncing off wobbling objects surrounded by blackness.

Panic called, but his chest muscles remained tight and still, while his arms and legs pushed in powerful bursts.

The cellar ended at a wall devoid of debris, but somewhere there had to be an opening for the water to pour in.

Flashing the light around brought the opening into view—one barely half of Gray's height and twice his width.

There wouldn't be room enough to swing his arms. Any descent through the enclosed cavern—who knew how far—was going to be slow and painful.

And already, pressure mounted in his lungs; his eyes stung. Any second, he'd pass out.

He swam and needled himself through the tunnel. The water pressure was higher here; he pumped burning legs harder—while the torch beam blurred and cleared, while his body screamed in agony.

Out there in the cove and ocean, his son awaited.

Three years couldn't have obliterated him entirely. Gray's baby had become an integral part of the sea, and maybe they should join here together. What was there in the world for him now? More failure as a father; more unrepentant criminals to hunt down. Did it all mean nothing in the end? Upon death, wouldn't he disappear into nothingness like Craig—except no one would mourn Gray. He didn't deserve it.

The tunnel ended and spilled out into the cove. The torch beam dispersed into nothingness, hitting no rock walls except the one behind him.

He reached for the hard edge but could feel nothing.

How much time had passed? Any second, he'd become delirious or unconscious. So little of his brain still functioned—but he knew one thing: the water was calmer down here than on the surface above. If he surfaced this close to the rocks, he'd be smashed to bits.

Should he crawl up the rock edge or swim further out? The pressure inside his chest had numbed, too. He no longer needed to breathe—only float under the surf until he reached Craig. And they'd be together forever. Noelle didn't know him, and Sita was half-way to finding her a new dad. Maybe it was time to let go finally.

A vice gripped his right wrist.

His entire body felt cut off from sensation—except at his scarred hand where the contact burned like a flame and pulled him up so hard his shoulder might dislocate.

It took everything to lift his head. Saltwater bubbled into his nostrils, the insides searing a little before going numb.

A small hand held on tight. Dead white feet and legs kicked vertically to lift them both upward. Gray wouldn't go. He couldn't leave Craig.

Trying to break free didn't work; the grip tightened further, scorching his skin until he almost screamed.

The apparition glowed.

A smiling face looked down with kind eyes and pointed upward with a small hand—and suddenly, the burning ceased.

Craig was here. Gray must go with his son. They wouldn't be parted, ever again.

Feet turned into meters, and they went up and up…while warmth through flooded Gray's. Craig looked so happy, so serene.

And now, the boy's face morphed into a little girl's. And Gray heard her cries—cries reminding him that a desperate killer still roamed the mansion, an unpredictable and out-of-control monster.

Craig pulled them up, higher and higher—where the current grew strong and whipped them in all directions.

Gray couldn't feel his legs, much less move them. He'd lost all control over his body, and now his lungs came back to life and created a vacuum in his chest, screaming for release.

Another few seconds—if he could stay conscious another few seconds, he could get to Noelle. But would that mean leaving his son?

Oh God, he couldn't do it. He couldn't let Craig be obliterated again by the sea.

The current came fiercely. Craig let go Gray's wrist and rested that bony hand on Gray's head,eyes calm and forgiving, for a second which might have lasted forever but soon went.

The boy's luminous body dissolved into blackness. Numbness receded and brought back a violent cold which clutched at the heart, tearing it to shreds.

No. No.

Don't go. I can't live without you. I don't know how I have for three years. Only by being numb, but now I'm not numb, and it's beyond pain—where consciousness drags you to a hell you can't endure. But maybe I can survive it, Craig, if I know you're somewhere okay. But I'll never know, will I? I'll never know for sure—until my dying day.

Gray's head broke the surface. He gulped in cold air and spray.

Shattered lungs convulsed and coughed, and like a rag doll, he flew amongst the white-tipped waves, bobbing up and down.

But oxygen worked its magic. All the empty blackness slowly filled with the sea's roar and the sensation of rain on his face.

He tried to gain control; the surf instead threw him against the rocks, and he hit his shoulder but felt no pain—only a crunching of bone against bone.

He had to swim out and find his son, who was out there somewhere. If only his body would move. If only reason hadn't reasserted itself, bringing the knowledge that nothing existed out there to find.

The next wave crashed on his head and pulled him out to sea before boomeranging him back against the rocks—this time into a crevice between two pointed boulders.

In a second, he'd be yanked out into the ocean again.

Gray roared as loud as he could and flung two lifeless arms together, linking them around a rock. But the tug was too strong. He couldn't hold on for much longer.

Shouting again only hurt her ears. They were the cries of a stranger.

Disjointed voices came from a distance. Gray's blurred eyes refocused and found movement in the rocks.

Teddy's round figure hobbled simian-like, balancing on both hands. "He's here! Hanging on. Quick, the tide will pull him out." Porch lights from a distance lit the Squire's haloed silhouette, but his face was a black void.

"Give me that rope." Seymour appeared out of nothingness. The wind knocked the doctor off his feet, and surf slashed across his face. "I'll tie it around him.

"And have us all pulled out? We form a chain. Emmy, wrap this around you."

Why had they all come? Gray's thinking cleared. They'd left Noelle alone with who—Sita, Lew, and Slope? What if the two smugglers returned for the painting? He shouted, but they didn't listen.

Seymour's scrunched face leaned in close. "He's cut. Careful—his neck or back might be broken."

"Hurry," Gray mouthed.

He floated upward and lay flat on rocks that dug into his back. An angry and curdled sky threatened to plummet upon them, but it was blocked by feminine hands hovering as though performing an incantation.

They encircling his neck. "I'm holding it steady," Emmy said. Her head sheltered his from the rain; her long hair fell forward in a semicircle, and water slid down their silky lengths.

An unknown force lifted him, and he floated towards the mansion, its shadowed turrets looming overhead in the power of the storm.

"You're going to be okay," Emmy said. Her forehead was serene. He believed her.

Everything numb started to feel warm. Seymour and Teddy were talking nearby while Gray floated towards the house. Their words jumbled into an unrecognizable blur.

Somehow, he had to stay awake—and yet the pull to close his eyes, for only a second, proved too much.

He'd close them for a second.

"Gray's passing out," someone said.

No, I'm not. Warmth flooded his arms and legs, and he was partly relieved to be alive, and in part wishing himself back in the sea—with that small and luminous hand upon his head.

Gray held on to that timeless moment, clutched at it so it would always be with him and never go.

Before everything went black.

CHAPTER TWENTY-FOUR

A VIOLENT PAIN smashed through the fog of his unconsciousness, accompanied by an excruciating snap, felt in his left shoulder.

Gray bolted up. "What the hell are you doing?"

Seymour held Gray's arm and shoulder. Emmy and Dad supported his torso.

The doctor shot him a look. "Don't move. Your shoulder was dislocated, and I've just replaced it in its socket. I didn't dare leave it dangling—in case you need your good arm tonight."

"You could have waited until I regained consciousness," Gray said. "You ever heard of pain control?"

"Sorry, James. I needed you awake, ASAP."

Seymour's dark look was shared by the other two. Across the salon, Slope and Sita worked at distracting a tired and crying Noelle. Teddy was with them.

Gray moved to get up, but Lew and Seymour held him down.

"She's okay, son. Your daughter's fine. Leave them for now."

"Yeah," Seymour chipped in. "The storm's not abating. It's still the middle of the night, in case you didn't know, and there's a killer loose among us. We needed you back if only to tell us what the hell is going on."

Gray ran a hand over his face. He now wore loose, dry clothes instead of his tux—Teddy's? The hearth roared a few feet away, sending sparks and welcome bursts of hot air.

Emmy hadn't said a thing, but her pale face and trembling lips told him she was at her breaking point.

Seymour spoke in bursts. Gray had never seen him this worked up. "I want to hear all about what happened at the cove, but first—I'm dying to know—who's the goddamn Stitcher?"

Gray rubbed his shoulder at the site of a bandage; his skin stung. He must have cut himself against the rocks, and the characteristic tug indicated Seymour had needed to stitch him up. At least the bones weren't broken.

"That's complicated. Someone get me something. I feel like I'm going to throw up."

Dad put a hand on his chest. "Take it easy. Lie back down."

"I don't want to. Some scotch—that might help."

Seymour made a face. Even at times of crisis, he was a character. "I'll get it, but not too much." He pointed a finger, clearly thrilled to have a live patient for a change. He returned a moment later with two fingers of single malt in a crystal tumbler—Gray's favorite.

It burned down his throat, brought life into his body.

Noelle had fallen back asleep across the room in her mother's arms. The shifting of a log as it crackled, the stillness of all eyes upon him, made time stand still. And it felt like Christmas for the first time this season, bringing a childhood bliss he scarcely remembered.

He wanted to hang onto it forever, but they were looking to him for answers.

211

Gray straightened and downed his scotch. "Where's Matisse?"

"He ain't the Stitcher." Teddy had joined them, jaw clenched, fists at his side. No one had lost more than this tough man—his fiancé and his adopted daughter. Still, he looked more angry than broken.

"No—and yes. Has anyone seen the boy?"

"Not since he ran off two hours ago."

Gray put down the glass and stood. The room blurred before clearing, and Seymour had both arms out in case he fell.

"Matisse locked me in the guest house cellar," Gray said. "I swam out through an old smuggler's cavern leading to the cove."

Lew's hand gripped his shoulder.

"I'm okay, Dad."

But Gray's thighs screamed. There must be bruises all over his body. He kept his expression neutral, feeling the doctor's eyes upon him.

Teddy shook his head. "No way Matisse killed my Farrah. He was with me the whole time after Farrah went off on her own. And we both found her afterward—lyin' dead on the terrace like that."

"He did kill his mother. I'll explain after we find him. Let's not forget we also have two violent fugitives on the property." Gray shook his head to clear his thinking. "Where's Vivienne."

"She went to the bathroom," Emmy said.

"Alone?"

Vivienne stepped into the room on cue. A purple and black lump adorned her forehead, and her lower lip looked like a grape.

"We've both looked better." She gave him a tight hug. "Mon Dieu, you frightened me. It's been a hell of a night."

"It's not over. Are you feeling well enough to help me search the house?"

She nodded and moved towards Slope.

Gray took Lew to one side. "You still have the revolver, in case either of the three return?"

"Yes." He leaned in, so only Gray could hear. "Who do I trust in this group?"

"Does Slope have his gun?"

"He says he didn't bring it to the party. Vivienne thinks he's head of the art smuggler's group." The Picasso rested against the nearby sofa.

"Not the head, but I can't exclude his involvement without interrogating the two thieves. They're on the property, and so is Matisse, thanks to the storm. We have to find him, at the very least, tonight. By morning, all three will have skipped town. Which means I have to decide whether to take Slope with me or leave him here."

"Take him—if only to get him the hell away from my granddaughter. And take Seymour, too. Emmy and I got it all covered."

"Watch Teddy," Gray said. Lew nodded before taking a seat beside a quiet and reflective Emmy. She no longer had the letter opener in her hand, but something told him it was nearby.

Seymour came up behind him, alongside Slope and Vivienne.

They moved upstairs to where he'd left Farrah's body. She lay undisturbed on the mattress in what must, coincidentally, have been her bedroom since another set of house keys was on the vanity, surrounded by perfumes, lotions and discarded jewelry. Gray stuck the extra set in the pocket of the oversized pants and further tightened the belt.

It took only a minute to locate Matisse. His weeping echoed down the hall. Whatever the boy was, he wasn't a natural killer—and his violence towards Farrah, not to mention Gray in the guest house, must have caught up with him.

Slope held them back with one hand and turned the knob.

Inch by inch, the door opened to reveal the sobbing, huddled form inside. Gray kneeled beside him.

"Where's Delilah?" he asked. "Did you leave her body in the guest house?"

The boy nodded. His red hair matched the bloodshot eyes; his face appeared raw and ruddy, as though from a lifetime of drinking and high blood pressure. And yet he was still a teenager with that haunted look—as though he could scarcely believe what had happened in the last few hours.

They split up. The remainder of the search upstairs revealed nothing.

Downstairs, the library and other rooms were empty. Gray even rechecked the basement, in case the two sailors had chosen that as a hiding place.

He and Seymour, towing a broken Matisse, returned to the back terrace and the French doors.

Outside, the storm raged, but the water level hadn't risen further.

Finding Delilah's body was imperative. They needed it as evidence to prove what might otherwise be impossible to prove.

He turned to Seymour. "The suture needle we found belonged to Farrah."

"Farrah?"

"She was the Stitcher."

"But—" The doctor pointed to Matisse. "He locked you in the cellar; he killed his mother, you said."

"The suturing on Farrah's mouth was rough and unevenly spaced. Emmy noticed, and so did I. We'd both witnessed Farrah's handiwork first hand with the first two victims, remember? She sutured precisely, almost professionally. Except she didn't leave the unused suture and needle behind with either of those victims. After Matisse killed her, he didn't know to take it with him." He turned to the boy. "You strangled her first. Do you remember doing it?"

"I don't know. I was mad." His wide eyes nearly popped out of his head. "She was going to leave with that Picasso that Grandfather left her. She loved that painting more than me."

His whole body shook.

Gray preferred to leave him indoors, but he wasn't about to let a man guilty of murder and attempted murder—all in one night—out of his sight. No matter how sorry he felt.

"No, wait a minute." Seymour clutched Gray's shoulder. "Teddy and Matisse found Farrah on the terrace together."

"The makeup, Doctor. Remember Farrah's face had makeup on it when you found her dead in the hall. One of the guests mentioned something tonight in passing: Farrah was a makeup artist in Vancouver, years ago. That's not just model, magazine eyeshadow we're talking about—it's special effects makeup. She made herself convincing as a victim; at least, convincing enough to compel Teddy and Matisse to run off and get help."

"I saw her after," Matisse cried. "I found her getting ready to leave. She was alive. She told me everything when I caught her in the act."

"And the suture?" Gray asked.

"She had it with her. Couldn't leave it behind, could she? The evidence had to go with her."

Slope came down the hall to join them, followed by Vivienne.

"Nothing," she said. "Stan and Diego aren't anywhere in the house."

Slope shook his head. "Impossible to say in a place this size. I guess you've been working undercover on my turf, Detective Caron. You might have told me."

Vivienne knew better than to take the bait. She clearly didn't trust Slope farther than she could throw him.

Grabbing Matisse's arm, Gray opened the terrace doors, squinted against the rain and wind. "I'll bet we find more than Delilah's body in that guest house. Stan and Diego, not to mention Butch, must be there. We've searched everywhere else."

In response, Slope pulled out his service revolver from his inside jacket pocket. "If they are, I'm prepared."

Vivienne caught Gray's eye, apparently sharing his trepidation. If Slope was part of the smuggling gang, would he silence the men before they could point any fingers? Or else silence Vivienne, Seymour, and Gray?

Together, they ran across the terrace and the drowned lawn to the chalet beyond—where a light shone through two square windows, giving it the smudged and incandescent appearance of watchful eyes.

Seymour was obviously anxious to get more answers. He yelled over the wind. "Why did Farrah kill that art critic?"

They were half-way to the cabin. Gray's legs cried out in pain, and he shouted back.

"He had that old snapshot of the Picasso because he knew Farrah's father had bought the painting—probably illegally, after the war. So much art went missing back then. And Donovan Price was commissioned to find it, I'm guessing.

216

Only he wanted it for himself. If he'd been an honest man instead of a crook, he'd be alive today."

"So he met Farrah and told her he wanted the painting."

"No. I believe Price met with her and later tried to kill her for the Picasso—where, I don't know—either in this guest house, or perhaps she has another place. Didn't you notice, Farrah has worn either pearls or turtlenecks for days, to conceal the bruises on her neck?"

Seymour looked confused.

"Remember, the old and new strangulation marks on her corpse?" Gray said. "She must have overpowered Donovan Price when he tried to kill her and strangled him instead."

"The cut on his neck!"

"From her diamond engagement ring. Yes."

Gray didn't bother to say the rest since Seymour was always fast on his feet—about Farrah copying the Stitcher's modus operand to divert suspicion towards a serial killer; about the poor babysitter who had died to solidify that pattern; and about Farrah's need to implicate both Emmy and the body farm, and to get rid of Delilah so that her fortune would revert back to Teddy.

They reached the guest house. Water filled the sunken entrance, and the front door lay off its hinges.

Slope took the lead, with Vivienne a foot behind him, ready to leap and grab the gun from his hand. Seymour held on to Matisse behind Gray.

Wading through the chest-deep water, they entered the house and immediately heard arguing coming from above—the kitchen, most likely. To the left, the cellar door lay off its hinges. It had lasted long enough for Gray to escape.

In a corner, Delilah's bloated and soaked corpse bobbed against the wall. Shaking his head, Seymour helped Gray carry

217

her up to the studio, where they gently placed her on the ground before quietly joining the others.

The storm's howling had concealed their footsteps.

Slope reached the kitchen entrance first, motioned those inside with his gun, and Stan, Diego, and Butch came out with their hands up.

Slope met Gray's eyes, looking like the cat who got the cream, while Vivienne tied the men's hands behind their backs with some rope she must have found in the house.

Ever resourceful Vivienne—she never let him down.

"I don't get one thing." Seymour kept his voice low. "Okay—two. Who headed the smuggling ring? Tell me it wasn't Slope, or we're in deep shit."

"Farrah led the gang," Vivienne said, tugging on the tied ropes harder than she needed to. "They all planned to sail away with the Picasso tonight. Isn't that so, boys? You had a big freak out after her dead body was found. I have the bruises to prove it."

Gray tried to pick up Delilah but swayed. With Vivienne covering the thugs, Slope and Seymour moved him aside and carried Delilah back to the house.

"Why did the victims have to disappear?" Seymour spat out the words, panting while wading through the water.

The world blurred and tilted. After all the night's strain, Gray couldn't collapse this short of seeing it all through. He found the energy to answer.

"So that no one would ask any questions when her body, too, disappeared. She set this up long ago when the babysitter disappeared. Teddy must have told her about the Stitcher killing fifteen years ago. Butch helped her with the bodies. I suspect he was more loyal to Farrah than to Teddy."

218

Once back at the house, everyone had more questions, and Gray answered them.

It seemed forever before they settled down and voluntarily withdrew to their assigned rooms.

Gray, meanwhile, took refuge in Teddy's library.

He sunk into the wingback chair, aching, exhausted and watched Noelle sleeping in his lap. Her hair felt soft; the tiny chest rose and fell, a look of complete peace on her face.

All the loose ends—the smugglers, that bloody painting which had cost so many lives—were Vivienne's and Slope's problem. All Gray wanted was to be with his daughter, and hang on to the wisps of Craig's imagined presence.

But even this precious moment was burdened. Gray would need to decide about Sita and whether he could be a better husband than he was before.

A twist in his gut provided the answer. They had both changed so much.

Shuffling from the hall interrupted his reverie.

Seymour and Emmy entered, with Seymour frowning at the glass of scotch beside Gray.

"You didn't pour me one?"

Gray put a finger to his lips. "She's asleep."

Seymour moved towards a drinks trolley and nodded at Emmy, but she declined.

"I have something to ask you," she said to Gray. "I know it isn't the best time. Maybe it can wait, but I have to know now."

Gray's heart didn't skip a beat. He felt no panic—only a numbness, inside and out.

Noelle didn't stir as he gently lifted and placed her in the nearby portable crib.

He watched her for a moment before sitting back down and rested his face in his hands.

Ice cubes rattled in the doctor's glass. "Emmy," he said. "Let it go."

Gray had done it—miraculously, he thought he'd solved the Stitcher murders without anyone digging up the past.

"You dated Mrs. Franklin's daughter, didn't you?" Emmy said.

He looked up. Emmy was wiping her damp hands on her dress and shaking.

In that drenched and stained taffeta dress, she looked like a girl who had missed her prom. Why hadn't someone offered her something else to wear? She must be cold and uncomfortable.

Whatever this was, it wasn't instigated in revenge for his initial rudeness towards her.

No—she wanted an answer to a question which plagued her, and she wanted it now. She had pegged Gray as one of the good guys and now wasn't sure.

"Mrs. Franklin didn't tell me you dated her daughter, Stacey; she must have been protecting you. But when we found Farrah's body, and you knew about the sutures being left at the crime scene fifteen years ago, I wondered how you knew."

Emmy paused a moment before continuing.

"Mrs. Franklin let that fact slip, but no one else seems to know about it—not Teddy, not your Dad, not even Slope. Slope was part of the tail end of that old investigation, even let me look at the police report, just to humor me. There's no mention of suture or instruments left at the site anywhere on those pages. You weren't part of the investigating team either."

"Doesn't mean James couldn't have found out," Seymour said. "Cops talk amongst themselves."

Gray held up a hand to stop Seymour. He'd made it so far without the whole thing unraveling.

But Emmy wasn't finished.

"I asked Teddy, tonight, if you knew the Franklins. He told me you dated Stacey for a year, loved her even. How did you know the suture was left beside her father's body all those years ago, Chief Inspector? Unless you were at the original crime scene yourself."

Silence fell upon the room.

Gray hadn't been himself since returning to Halfmoon Bay, but in the last few days a door had opened up.

He could let go the need to control things – Noelle breathed deeply, still asleep nearby – and know that what was authentically his, would remain.

Even the storm outside had eased. The sea now rose and fell more smoothly; its cobalt depths a little less lonely, dawn peeking through over the horizon in emerging layers of white, blue, orange, and pink.

He felt like himself, whatever that strange mix of calm and obsession was – it worked for him.

Seymour grew redder by the second, but his face registered no questions or surprise. He moved to Emmy, lowering his voice but enough of it traveled across the room.

"Don't do this. You don't know—"

"I know enough. And why do you always protect him? Didn't he kill his son; wasn't he at least partly responsible for that?"

"What happened fifteen years ago isn't the same as what occurred with his son. His son's tragedy might have been prevented."

"I agree."

"But listen to me. I know the details of the old Stitcher case. I made it my business to know and find out from the highest quarters. James isn't the guilty party. He's not the culprit; he's not a victim – he's the hero. The first victim, Ronald Franklin, was an extraordinarily ill-dispositioned man, secretly feared by his family."

"A hero?" Emmy said. "Are you joking?"

Seymour moved towards the trembling woman who had reached her limit. "He's one of the good guys—believe me."

Nothing would be hidden now, from the world or himself. Gray breathed in and out. He had a choice and could be himself again. But first, the protective hand had to be removed from the wound. Exposing it to the onslaught.

"Why should I believe you?" Emmy said. "You follow him around like a puppy."

Seymour stiffened. "A puppy with some wit and charm, I should hope."

She held herself tight and glared at Gray as he approached.

"Enough," Gray said. "You're right."

Seymour opened his mouth to speak.

Gray shook his head. "It's time, my friend."

A dense and perpetual knot within Gray's chest unraveled as the words formed on his bruised lips; things finally said, finally out in the open.

"I'm the original Stitcher from fifteen years ago, Emmy. I killed Ronald Franklin. And I take full responsibility."

Her eyes grew wet and sharp. Seymour looked past Gray with pressed lips and a desperate hand shot up in warning.

Emmy's head turned first at the sound of a firm, closing click—towards where Slope stood at the doorway with his hand on the knob. How long had he been there?

"That's mighty interesting," Slope said. "Mighty interesting, indeed."

His entrance woke Noelle, and seeing the sergeant, her sleep-moistened face grew fiercely red, the round mouth opened to form a circle, and following a pregnant pause, her ear-piercing wail shot across the room.

THE END OF BOOK 2

BOOK 3~COMING SOON!
FOR BOOK 3 EXCLUSIVE PROMOTIONAL PRICE AND RELEASE DATE, AND EXCLUSIVE PEEKS—INCLUDING GRAY'S ACCIDENT SCENE WHERE HE LOST HIS SON, AND OTHER DELETED SCENES:

GRAY JAMES: BOOK 3
SUBSCRIBE At
www.rituwrites.com

EXCERPT FROM AMAZON BESTSELLER, *HIS HAND IN THE STORM*, BOOK 1
DOWNLOAD FOR FREE HERE

MORE NUMBING PAIN.

At precisely five-thirty am on April the first, Chief Inspector Gray James tucked his cold hands into his pockets, straightened his spine, and looked up.

He breathed out through his nose, warm breath fogging the air as if jettisoning out of a dragon and tried to dispel the

223

mingled hints of flesh, cherry blossoms, and the raw, living scent of the river.

The drumming of his heart rang deep in his chest – brought on more by intellectual excitement than any visceral reaction to murder. Because of this, Gray accepted an atavistic personal truth.

He needed this case like he'd needed the one prior, and the one before that. That someone had to die to facilitate this objectionable fix bothered him, but he'd give audience to that later. Much later.

A car backfired on le Chemin Bord Ouest, running east-west along Montreal's urban beach park. A second later, silence ensued, save the grievous howling of a keen eastwardly wind, and the pendulating creak of nylon against wood, back and forth, and back and forth.

Heavy boots tromping through the snow and slush came up from behind. A man approached. Tall, but not as tall as Gray, his cord pants and rumpled tweed conveyed the aura of an absent-minded professor, yet the shrewd eyes – not malicious, but not categorically beneficent either – corrected that impression.

Forensic Pathologist John Seymour looked up at the body hanging from the branch of a grand oak, gave it the eye and said, "Well, I can tell you one thing right off."

"What's that?"

"You wouldn't be caught dead in that suit."

Gray sighed. "What do you suggest? That I refer the victim to my tailor?" To which Seymour shrugged and got to work.

With every creak of the rope biting into the tree's bough, Gray half-expected the swinging shoes to brush the snow-laden grass; each time the cap-toed oxfords narrowly missed. A grease stain marked the bony protrusion of the left white sock (with a corresponding scuff on the heel – from being dragged?) above which the crumpled brown wool-blend fabric of the pants and ill-fitting jacket rippled in the wind – like the white-tipped surface of the river beyond.

Dawn cast a blue light on the water and snow. A damp cold sank through his coat and into his bones. Amazing how the usually peaceful beach park took on a menacing air: the St. Lawrence choppier than usual, swirls of sand and snow rolling like tumbleweeds, the sky heavy and low. But a children's playground lay behind the hanging body, and its red swings, bright yellow slide, and empty wading pool offered a marked contrast to the swaying corpse.

With every flash, Scene of Crime Officers photographed the body and documented what remained: only an exposed skull, framed by sparse hair on top, ears on either side, and a wrinkly neck puckered in a noose. A red silk tie under the hangman's knot only accentuated the complete absence of blood. Blood would have been preferable. The features were stripped to the bone with eroded teeth set in a perpetual grin as if the skull were enjoying a joke at everyone's expense.

"White male in his early fifties," Seymour said. "Well off, by the look of him. Only small bits of tissue left on the cheekbones, lips and around the eyes. Notice the distinctive gap between the two front teeth."

That could help with identification. The customized ringtone on Gray's cel played "She's Always a Woman." Why was she calling him so soon? He stabbed the phone and tucked it back into his cashmere coat pocket before circling the body several times.

"What killed him?" Gray asked.

"The facial trauma preceded the hanging."

That much was obvious since the rope wasn't eaten away like the face.

"We can't know the cause of death until I get him on the slab," Seymour said. "And before you ask, the time of death is hard to say. Parts of him are already frozen. Maybe four to seven hours ago. I'll have a better window after I've checked the stomach contents and what's left of the eyes."

Seymour crouched and felt the victim's knees and lower legs. "Rigor mortis has set in, probably sped up by the cold." He rotated the stiff ankles. "Look at these tiny feet. Can't have been too popular with the ladies."

Gray closed his eyes and counted to five.

All around, professionals bustled gathering evidence, clearing onlookers and photographing the scene. The park lay sandwiched between the beach and parking lot leading to the main road. On one side, the river flowed eastward in a blue-gray haze, blurring the line between water and sky. On the other, traffic going into downtown Montreal grew heavier by the minute. The road led to his neighborhood, where Victorian and Edwardian homes, bistros, and cafés crunched together for ten hipster-infused blocks.

This park held memories of weekends spent with his wife and son. A lifetime ago. *Why did it have to happen here, of all places?*

"Did some kind of acid cause the burns?" he asked.

"Yeah. Parts of the eyes are still there. Almost as if they were left for last. I wonder why."

Gray could think of a reason but didn't elaborate.

A gust of wind swung the corpse's legs sideways, narrowly missing an officer's head.

"What the hell." Seymour grabbed the ankles. "The sooner we cut him down, the better."

226

Which couldn't be soon enough. Gray bent down and held the lower legs. He gripped the ankle awkwardly with his right thumb and little finger, the middle three immobile these last three years since the accident, and a snake-like scar running from his palm to his wrist blanched from the cold.

Despite his hanging on tight, the corpse danced in the wind. "Don't rush on my account, Doctor."

Finally, attendants cut the victim down and laid him on a stretcher. The doctor hunched over, his blond hair parting in the breeze revealing a pink, flaky scalp, the grinning corpse powerless to refuse examination.

"Definitely acid," Seymour said. "Going to be hard for you to trace, since it's so easy to get. Impure sulphuric acid's available at any mechanic shop. You find the purer kind in pharmaceuticals." He flashed a penlight into the facial crevices and probed them with a long, needle-like instrument.

The victim couldn't feel it, but each stab and scrape made Gray flinch. "Must you do that?"

"Look at these chipped bones," Seymour said. "Here, next to the supraorbital foramen, and here on the left zygomatic arch. They're edged off, not dissolved by acid."

"Torture, right?"

"Could be."

Gray paced his next six words: "Was he alive for the acid?"

"I'm going to have to brush up on vitriolage. If he were, he'd have breathed it in, and we'd see scarring in the esophagus, nostrils, and lungs."

Looking around at the flat, deserted beach park, the ropy ebb and flow of the water, Gray said, "He didn't die here, did he?"

"No. From what I can see, livor mortis indicates he probably died sitting and was strung up later. I'll let you know after all his clothes are off." Seymour pushed himself up with his hands, his knees popping like the report of a firearm. "What could the poor bastard have done to deserve this?"

Gray didn't answer. As someone guilty of the greatest sin of all, he considered himself wholly unqualified to make any such judgment.

His cel played "She's Always a Woman," again, and he pulled it out. Images from the previous night played in his mind: her hands flat on the mattress, his palm encircling her belly from behind. And those unexpectedly strong martinis she'd made earlier.

Putting away the phone, he spoke brusquely. "When will you have something ready?"

"Preliminary report probably later today. And I'll send remnants of the acid for analysis to determine the type and grade."

As the body was carried to a van and Seymour followed, second-in-command Lieutenant Vivienne Caron approached Gray carrying two small cups of espresso from a nearby Italian café. Wonderful steam rose from the opened lids, and the dark, nutty aroma drifted forward, the first hint of comfort on this bleak morning.

Warmth exuded from her chocolate brown eyes – eyes both direct and shy, their color perfectly matching her short, straight tresses now whipping about in the wind and framing gentle features.

"Chief Inspector." She addressed him formally, despite their longstanding friendship. The sound of her nearly perfect English was pleasant and familiar, beautifully accented with the musical intonations characteristic of certain Québecois.

Even though she held the coffee before his left hand; he grasped it awkwardly with his right.

"Don't spill any on that thousand-dollar suit," she said.

It made him gag. "Why do you always add so much sugar?"

"Because I know with a juicy case to solve, you'll be too busy to eat or sleep."

A moment of silence passed between them, pregnant with history he didn't want exhumed.

"I have to make sure you're okay," she said. "Even if you refuse to... She was my best friend."

He placed a hand on her shoulder. "You live with Sita's ghost more than I do. Enough time has passed for me."

"Maybe. It's changed you."

"For the worse?"

Vivienne stilled, her mouth open. "Non. For the better. That's the problem."

Her eyes were warm yet part adversarial. He saw it as the conflicting desire of wanting him to be okay, but not to leave her to grieve alone. She'd once told him the same trauma that had disillusioned her had enlightened him.

"It doesn't matter what happens," he whispered.

"Doesn't matter?" Her voice took on an edge.

"As long as you can control your reactions – it doesn't matter. Freedom comes from living in grays – no black; no white. No convenient polarities."

Her eyes pierced his, but he knew, out of her respect, she wouldn't directly say what she thought. That he oscillated between Zen and obsession, contentment and blackness.

She shuffled her feet. "I don't know how you made that leap, after the tragedy."

"The worst thing that could ever happen to me has happened. After that, I can either fear everything or nothing – I have nothing left to lose."

Vivienne said nothing.

What right had he to lecture her when he still experienced unguarded moments which terrorized him, filled his insides with quicksand as that malignant though raced through his mind: what do I do now? How do I fill this day and twenty years of interminable days when everything is for nothing? When this life feels surreal, dissociated as though I'm on a foreign planet with strangers.

Those moments often occurred when he didn't have a case; they occurred before sleep and drove his nightly obsession.

"Living in Gray?" Vivienne shook her pretty head. "I believe in good and evil."

"Then where do I fall? Or will you make excuses for me?"

"Non. I won't make excuses for you. "

Her eyes hooded over; she took a step back. A door slammed between them, again.

"No cel phone, no ID," she said. "Any footprints or tracks are covered by snow."

"Let's have someone check with the occupants of the hospital rooms facing the river."

Westborough Hospital sat directly across the road. A magnificent feat of engineering, its four glass-walled buildings were connected by skyways. It had taken twenty years of fundraising to build (with its founding director recently fleeing to Nicaragua under allegations of embezzling some of those funds) and took up several square blocks.

Gray forced down the coffee. Already, warmth and caffeine coursed through his system, bringing life to his numb toes inside the slush-soaked loafers. "Did you check with missing persons?"

"Only one recent report matches. Norman Everett of Rosedale Avenue in Upper Westmount. He's only been gone since last night and reported missing by his step-son, Simon

Everett. And of note, Norman's a doctor at Westborough Hospital."

Gray's head shot up. "Missing since last night, and works at this particular hospital? The timing's perfect. Give me his details. I'll do the interview myself while you finish up here."

"D'accord."

She gave him the number, and he made the call to Norman Everett's house, reaching the missing man's wife, Gabrielle.

Before she could go, a Scene of Crime Officer jumped forward and handed Gray a transparent evidence bag.

"Found this by the tree over there, Chief."

"How recent?"

"It lay just under the snow. The city cleaned this area recently; hardly any debris around."

Gray thanked him and looked down at the four by six-inch identity badge, examined the photo, and read the identifying details, gripping it tight enough that his fist blanched. The image blurred for the briefest second before clearing.

Vivienne rubbed her hands together. "What's wrong?" He didn't trust his voice yet. A shoal of uncertainties flooded his chest. The case suddenly became more raw, more urgent, but he'd handle it. He always did. Gray unclenched his jaw and fingers, and handed her the evidence bag.

"The killer?"

"A witness."

"Look at that ID," Vivienne said. "Look what it says. You can't be sure."

"Yes, I can." His tone came out harsher than he'd intended. He could guess her next words, and he'd deserve them. *Does anything matter, now? Will you be able to control your reactions?* But she didn't say it. Didn't point out the one circumstance that sliced

231

his calm with the efficiency of a scalpel. Instead, she met his eyes in a gentle embrace before moving farther up the beach.

Bells sounded from St. Francis, the eighteenth-century cathedral up the road for Angelus prayer. Québec had the largest Catholic population in the country, and maybe as a result, the lowest church attendance and marriage rate. But the familiar ringing comforted and smoothed the sharp edges of his morning.

Gray left the cordoned off area, crossed the breadth of the beach park and headed to the attached parking lot and his car; the black metallic exterior gleamed in the distance.

At one time, the Audi S5 consumed a substantial chunk of his detective's salary, but he hadn't cared. Memories of countless family road trips lay etched within its metal frame.

Still twenty feet away, he pressed the automatic start to warm the engine, just as Seymour summoned him from behind.

The doctor jogged over sporting a wry smile, breath steaming in the cold air, and his long coat flapping. Behind him, the van carrying the body left the parking lot.

"I forgot to ask you earlier – about your next expedition," Seymour said. "Mind having some company?"

"I failed last time," Gray said. "Or hadn't you heard?"

"A fourteen-hundred-kilometer trek to the South Pole, on foot, is hardly a failure."

"It is if you can't make the journey back. Anyway–"

A boom drowned out his words. The earth shook, and air blasted towards them, throwing Gray to the ground onto his right shoulder, pain searing up his arm. Chunks of metal and debris flew from the newly obliterated Audi in every direction, denting nearby cars and clanging against the pavement. A puff of smoke shot upward, chasing the flames, leaving the smell of burning rubber and metal hanging in a thick cloud – while cars on the nearby road screeched to a sudden halt. The fire swayed as though alive, angry arms flailing and crackling, spitting sparks in all directions.

"What the hell!" Seymour lay in the snow, his mouth open, his arm up to ward off the scorching heat.

Gray's car lay mutilated, the black paint graying as it burned. People jumped out of their cars to take a look. Vivienne and some officers ran towards him, their feet pounding on the asphalt.

"Someone is damn pissed off at you," Seymour said, eying his own dented Mercedes. He turned to Gray. "What did you do?"

ONCE AGAIN, GABRIELLE EVERETT couldn't find her husband. He hadn't come home the previous night, and she didn't know where he was. Truth be told, this was the second one she'd lost. As Oscar Wilde would have said: to lose the first could be attributed to bad luck, but to lose a second was surely akin to carelessness. No longer in the throes of romantic love (she remained open to it; it was love that did not return the favor), she nevertheless believed in keeping a hold of one's spouse. And here she was, having lost another one.

The first had gone missing ten years earlier in the Jean-Talon Market and never been heard from again. Gabi presumed he'd run away from his life as a lawyer, more than he'd run away from her, and could only hope it didn't reflect too harshly on her public image.

Despite her Francophone beginnings below the railway tracks, she now lived in the affluent Anglo neighborhood of

Westmount, where one was expected to keep the front garden professionally tended, and one's reputation for austerity and predictability intact. Here, a four-way stop sign meant the grander car had the right of way, and scandal and discontent were best left blanketed under the carpet of one's Mercedes.

Gabi closed her eyes and took a deep breath. Entering the kitchen, she decided to make a cappuccino. The freshly ground beans scented the air. Today, she poured frothed milk into a simple leaf design, though, in her barista days, she could have favored a swan, a butterfly, or even the face of a bulldog.

The empty day stretched before her. As did the empty house. The living room looked staged, as though tarted up for a quick sale; so different from the apartment she lived in when she was ten, where the air stank of dirty dishes and laundry drying on the radiator. Where the smell of mold and dead mice was the norm. Where on that fateful day, with a father who had recently died and a mother lying on the sofa in a drunken stupor, Gabi had frantically searched for the life-saving object – the medicine – that fateful moment when Gabi had learned what it meant to have nothing left to lose. And she'd never forgotten. Money helped. Becoming a monster helped.

Today, in her Westmount house, holding the steaming cup between cold hands, she stepped out onto the porch.

The crisp breeze gained momentum, carrying with it the sweet promise of spring as it swept across Georgian and Tudor-style manors lining the affluent hilltop. She breathed in deeply, washing away old memories and old remembered smells of mold and mice.

A figure caught her eye, coming out from behind a cherry tree. It bore an uncensored look of violence and contempt. The face seemed familiar, just at the edge of Gabi's recollection – familiar, yet changed.

She scurried back into the house, slammed the door, and snapped the bolt in place. Recognition just within reach, she peered out the window for another glimpse and saw that the figure stood still, seemingly chiseled in granite.

And then it came to her: her husband, Norman, had revealed something while drinking – something regarding the health tech startup her son, Simon, had launched two years earlier, and in which Norman functioned as Medical Adviser. The company was poised to sell for hundreds of millions, and for Gabi, nothing mattered more than Simon. Nothing.

The links fit together in a chain of events. More were coming – it wasn't over. All the faces concerned flashed in Gabi's mind – of all the people involved, including the remembered face of her beloved little frail sister.

A shrill pierced the air and made her drop the cup. Coffee spilled onto the Persian. The phone kept ringing as the brown liquid spread and sank into the weave, the stain staring up at her, spoiling the perfection of her professionally decorated foyer.

She lifted the receiver. A baritone voice on the other end, smooth as cognac, eased her strain. Until he identified himself.

"Mrs. Everett?"

"Yes?"

"This is Chief Inspector Gray James of the SPVM. Your son reported your husband, Norman Everett, missing. Could I come and see you right away?"

Simon had done what? Already? Stupid boy. She swallowed the dry lump in her throat and pushed out the words. "Yes. I'm home now." Of course, she was home. He'd telephoned the house, hadn't he? The policeman thanked her and said he'd be over shortly.

Ending the call, Gabi peeked out the window. The figure had gone.

Thick clouds scurried overhead, blocking the sun and darkening the sky. An arc of light streamed in through the foyer window onto the rug, gradually narrowing to a sliver until it finally disappeared and she could no longer discern the coffee stain.

Her thoughts flew to her son. How could she protect him? From violence, from failure, from the arid clutches of poverty Gabi had once known so well herself?

But Gabi understood that the most dangerous person in the world was someone with nothing left to lose.

And she knew, in that instant, that her second husband would never come home.

DOWNLOAD BOOK 1 FOR FREE ON AMAZON

SUBSCRIBE TO GET PROMO PRICE ON BOOK 3

www.rituwrites.com

ABOUT THE AUTHOR

Ritu Sethi needs coffee, beaches, and murder mysteries to survive – not necessarily in that order. She won the Colorado Gold Award for the first in the Chief Inspector Gray James Murder Mystery Series, *His Hand In the Storm*. The book was also a Daphne du Maurier Suspense finalist and an Amazon Kindle Free Bestseller.

Right now, she's fulfilling her lifelong desire of becoming a mystery writer. Many thanks to all the readers who are making that possible.

www.rituwrites.com

Facebook: @ritusethiauthor
Twitter: @ritusethiauthor
Amazon: https://www.amazon.com/author/ritusethi
Bookbub: https://www.bookbub.com/authors/ritu-sethi?follow=true

Made in the USA
Las Vegas, NV
31 January 2021

16892567R00142